TALES FOR HALLOWEEN

A.F. SORIA

TALES FOR HALLOWEEN

A.F. SORIA

On the night of All Souls' Day, I was awakened at I don't know what time by the ringing of the bells; their monotonous and eternal tolling brought to my mind this tradition that I heard recently in Soria.

Gustavo Adolfo Bécquer, 'The Mount of the Souls'.

Darkness there, and nothing more.

Edgar Allan Poe, 'The Raven'.

Welcome to my house. Come freely. Go safely; and leave something of the happiness you bring!

Bram Stoker, 'Dracula'.

CONTENTS

Introduction

Halloween is a holiday with deep historical and cultural roots. Its origins lie in a mixture of Celtic, Roman and Christian traditions.

The beginnings of Halloween can be traced back to the Celtic festival of Samhain, which marked the end of summer and the beginning of winter in Ireland, as well as in the UK, parts of France and Spain.

The Celts believed that during Samhain, the line between the world of the living and the dead was blurred, allowing spirits to return to Earth. To appease the spirits and predict the future, Druids performed rituals and lit bonfires.

The expansion of the Roman Empire brought about the fusion of Celtic and Roman traditions. The festival of Pomona, dedicated to the goddess of fruit and orchards, was celebrated at the same time as Samhain. This fusion contributed to the adoption of elements such as apples, which became a symbol of Halloween.

In the 7th century, the Catholic Church introduced All Saints' Day on 1 November, followed by All Souls' Day on 2 November. These festivities sought to replace pagan beliefs and honour the saints and the dead. The eve of All Saints' Day, called All Hallows' Eve, was later shortened to Halloween.

With the arrival of European settlers in America, they brought their traditions with them, including Halloween. Over the centuries, the holiday was mixed with Native American influences, giving rise to unique celebrations. Traditions such as pumpkin carving, trick-or-treating and ghost stories have flourished.

Illuminated pumpkins, or jack-o'-lanterns, originated from an Irish legend about a rogue named Jack who tricked the devil. Pumpkins were not used in the beginning, but turnips. In ancient Scotland and elsewhere, it was believed that bachelors could see the face of their future spouse if they performed special rituals on Halloween.

Halloween is a holiday that has evolved over the centuries and remains a mystery and a source of fun for people of all ages around the world. Its rich and varied history has contributed to making it one of the most iconic festivities of the year. In parts of Spain they celebrate Samaín, as a way of honouring their Celtic roots. Other cultures have their own similar festivities, such as the Day of the Dead in Mexico, Chuseok in Korea or Obon in Japan, all of which are marked by the veneration of ancestors and the recognition of the transition between life and death.

The last night in the cursed forest

In a small village in Black Forest, Halloween was celebrated with great enthusiasm. Children dressed in costumes asked for sweets from door to door while the adults told scary stories around bonfires. Of all the local legends, the one about the cursed forest was feared the most.

Elise and Hans, two young adventurers, listened attentively as the old man Otto told the grisly tale. According to him, the Witch of the Forest had cast a curse over the place, and all who entered its shadows were trapped forever, doomed to wander like lost spirits.

Despite the warnings, Elise was irresistibly curious about the cursed forest. After all, she had always considered scary stories to be mere fabrications.

Determined to unravel the mystery, she challenged Hans to accompany her on a night-time expedition.

As night fell, the two friends ventured deep into the forest, guided only by the light of their lanterns and the courage in their hearts. The thick foliage and twisted branches of the trees seemed to come alive with every step they took, as darkness enveloped them.

Unexpectedly, a pale, ethereal figure emerged from the shadows, interrupting their advance. It was Emma, the girl who had disappeared in the forest many years ago. Terrified but intrigued, they decided to help her, and followed her into the depths of the cursed forest, unaware that they were about to face the most terrifying night of their lives.

Emma, looking ghostly, led them through the maze of trees and shadows. As they advanced, the strange whispers filtering through the branches seemed to increase in intensity. The atmosphere became more and more oppressive, making the youths breathing heavier and their steps slower.

On the spur of the moment, Emma stopped in front of an old ivy-covered hut, almost consumed by nature. In a faint, mournful voice, she explained that the Witch of the Forest lived there, the only one who could free her from her eternal suffering. However, she warned them not to look directly into the eyes of the Witch, for her gaze was capable of devouring the souls of mortals.

Dismayed, they entered the hut. Inside, the gloom was interrupted by the faint glow of slowly burning candles. And there, in the middle of the room, stood the Witch, wrapped in a dark cloak that barely revealed her face.

Armed with courage, they begged the Witch to free Emma and break the curse of the forest. The Witch agreed in exchange for a price: a night in the cursed forest, facing their worst fears. Though scared, they accepted the deal, willing to prove their worth and save the poor girl. After telling them how to break the spell, the Witch disappeared in a whirlwind of shadows, leaving them alone in the darkness.

With the disappearance of the Witch, the hut was plunged into almost total darkness. Elise and Hans, with their hearts pounding, left the hut and walked back into the forest, accompanied by Emma's ethereal silhouette.

At first, the ordeal seemed straightforward. However, as they went on, the whispers of the forest turned to wailing and piercing screams coming from all directions. The young people hugged each other tightly, struggling not to panic.

All of a sudden, the shadows of the forest came to life, taking the shapes of their worst nightmares.

For Elise, the shadows became poisonous snakes that slithered along the ground and coiled around her, while for Hans, the shadows took the form of deformed, monstrous creatures that pursued him with an unquenchable thirst for blood.

Though terrified, they realised they had to face their fears if they were to free Emma and survive the night. In an act of bravery, they confronted the shadows, shouting at them that they were not real and could not harm them.

Gradually, the shadows began to dissipate, and the screams and wails faded into thin air. Exhausted, they continued on their way through the cursed forest, aware that the ordeal was not yet over.

The three finally reached a clearing in the forest, where a circle of stones carved with mystical symbols stood in the darkness. The full moon was glowing reddish, bathing the place in an ominous light.

Both youths stood in the centre of the stone circle, while Emma stood beside them, motionless. Following the instructions the Witch had given them before she disappeared, Elise and Hans began to recite aloud an ancient incantation that was to break the curse.

As their voices echoed in the clearing, the wind began to blow more strongly, and the shadows of the forest seemed to come alive once more. With a lump in their throats, they continued to recite the incantation, feeling the mystical power enveloping them.

Suddenly, a flash of lightning illuminated the night sky, followed by a deafening clap of thunder. Emma's figure began to tremble and glow with an intense light, while the shadows around her writhed and shrieked in agony.

Elise and Hans spoke the last words of the spell, and Emma's figure exploded in a torrent of light that illuminated the entire forest.

At the same time, the shadows disintegrated into nothingness, leaving the air filled with a sepulchral silence.

With the disappearance of the shadows, they both remained in the stone circle, trying to catch their breath. The red moon slowly faded, returning its silvery glow to the night. But something didn't feel quite right.

Unexpectedly, a cold, sinister laugh echoed through the forest. The Witch had returned, emerging from the shadows that still clung to the trees. Her expression was one of triumph and malice.

'You naive!' exclaimed the Witch. 'You believed you had released poor Emma, but in reality you have released the real curse that lay dormant in the heart of the forest.'

Elise and Hans felt indescribable terror at her words. The Witch went on to explain that the spell they had recited not only freed Emma, but also awakened an ancient, dark power that had lain dormant for centuries. The ground began to tremble, and out of the earth rose a monstrous creature, made of shadows and hatred. Its presence was so overwhelming that it seemed to consume all hope around it. The Witch laughed maliciously as she watched the beast rise before them.

'Now, young fools, your fate is sealed,' said the Witch. 'Tonight, the cursed forest will take its toll.'

Elise and Hans, terrified, hugged each other tightly as the creature approached them, and the shadows swirled in a macabre dance. The last night in the cursed forest had come to its terrible and frightening end.

The shadow of the abyss

Manila, 1890. The city was bustling with activity as carriages drove through the cobblestone streets of Intramuros, the walled district. In a luxurious house on Calle Real, Don Esteban Montenegro, a wealthy Spanish merchant, was preparing for a grand party in honour of his wife, Catalina. The Filipino lady had been feeling unwell for some time and her husband wanted to cheer her up. The mansion was filled with exotic flowers and the guests, dressed in their finest clothes, commented on the beauty of the house and the splendid hospitality of the Montenegro family.

Catalina, elegantly dressed in a white lace gown, walked through the halls, smiling politely at the guests while her heart pounded uneasily. A shiver ran down her spine, as if an invisible presence was watching her.

Shaking her head, she attributed her discomfort to nerves and concentrated on being the perfect hostess.

In the library, Father Alejandro, the new priest, was chatting animatedly with Don Esteban. However, he couldn't help noticing the anguish in Catalina's eyes every time she passed through the door. Father Alejandro felt a strange connection with the young lady and decided to approach her to offer words of comfort:

'Doña Catalina, this is a truly magnificent party. But it seems to me that something is bothering you. Are you all right?'
'Father Alejandro, it is kind of you to be concerned. I am grateful for your presence here tonight. I must admit that I feel uneasy, as if something dark lurks in the shadows of this mansion.'
'I understand that large meetings can be overwhelming, but sometimes our intuition can guide us. Have you felt anything more specific, anything that has particularly disturbed you?'
'It's hard to explain, Father. But sometimes I feel as if an invisible presence is watching me and I think I hear whispers.'
'That is intriguing. Perhaps I could meditate on it. Perhaps there is a reasonable explanation for your sensations. And of course, don't forget to pray. In prayer we can find solace for our tribulations.'
'Yes, Father Alejandro, I will. I appreciate your help and your understanding.'

The party continued late into the night, but the festive atmosphere could not dispel Catalina's growing restlessness. When she finally retreated to her bedroom, her ears picked up barely audible whispers from the shadows. With each step she took in the direction of her alcove, the whispers intensified, as if an invisible crowd was murmuring around her.

Catalina lit all the candles in the room, but the shadows seemed to stalk her from the corners, dancing and writhing on the walls. Desperate, she fell to her knees and began to pray, asking the Virgin Mary for protection. The whispering stopped momentarily, but the presence remained, as if waiting for the right moment to strike.

The next morning, Catalina shared her fears with Father Alejandro, who was concerned for the young lady. He decided to investigate the Montenegro mansion and its history, suspecting that there was something dark lurking in its corridors. Catalina, grateful for the priest's help, felt a little calmer, although the shadows and whispers continued to haunt her.

Father Alejandro delved into the history of the Montenegro mansion. Going through the municipal archives, he discovered that the mansion had been built on the ruins of an old hospital that was destroyed by a mysterious fire more than a century ago. Intrigued by this information, the priest began to search for historical records and testimonies of people who had lived near the hospital before its destruction.

Isidro, the loyal Filipino butler of the Montenegro, cautiously observed the priest's growing interest in the affairs of the house. Fearing that the dark secrets of the mansion's past would be discovered, Isidro vowed to protect his patrons at any cost, even if it meant facing the Shadow of the Abyss and its terrible consequences.

In the mansion, Catalina continued to be tormented by whispers and shadows that seemed to be drawing ever closer. On one occasion, she was alone in the main hall when a dark figure passed quickly in front of her, leaving behind a trail of intense cold. Terrified, she locked herself in her room and prayed fervently for her safety.

On the evening of the third day after the party, Father Alejandro visited the outskirts of Intramuros. The local elders told him of an ancient legend about a dark abyss that supposedly lay beneath the old hospital, a portal to the underworld for those who perished there, but from which terrible creatures and evil spirits also emerged.

Concerned for Catalina's safety and his own soul, he decided to share with Don Esteban the information he had discovered.

However, the merchant was sceptical and preferred to discuss with the doctors the illness that was affecting his wife, who was behaving stranger by the day, speaking unknown languages that she could not possibly have learned on her own and showing unusual strength.

Isidro was following Father Alejandro's investigations closely. The servant, fearing that the priest might unleash an even greater evil by trying to confront the Shadow of the Abyss, decided to take desperate measures to protect the Montenegro family and his own secrets.

On the fourth night, while Catalina was trying to pray in her room, Isidro crept into Don Esteban's study and searched for an ancient book of rituals that had been passed down through generations in his family. He knew that within its pages were the secrets to keeping the Shadow of the Abyss at bay, but he also knew that the price to be paid for such knowledge would be high.

Isidro studied the ancient book and performed a dark ritual in the basement of the mansion, hoping to appease the Shadow of the Abyss and prevent it from continuing to torment Catalina. However, in doing so, the butler involuntarily released other dark entities that had been trapped in the abyss for centuries.

As Isidro delved into the world of dark rituals, Father Alejandro was going through his books on how to perform an exorcism and house blessings. He had a plan to confront the Shadow of the Abyss and save Catalina from her growing terror. But a solemn exorcism can only be performed by a bishop or a priest with the bishop's permission. In these cases it is necessary to proceed with prudence, by strictly observing the rules established by the Church.

Father Alejandro obtained permission from the bishop, arranged his prayers and blessed the water to expel the demons that were lurking in the Montenegro mansion and possessing Catalina.

That same stormy afternoon, Catalina confessed to Father Alejandro that the whispers and shadows had increased in intensity and frequency, that at times she did not feel in control of herself, and that she feared for her life. The priest, determined to protect the young lady, convinced Don Esteban to allow him to perform an exorcism ceremony in the mansion, assuring him that this would put an end to the curse that seemed to have fallen on the house and his wife. Although concerned about the possible consequences, he reluctantly agreed to the priest's request, as he also wished to protect Catalina, who could not be cured by the best doctors his fortune could afford.

On the night of the exorcism, everyone gathered in the main hall of the mansion, where the priest began to recite the holy scriptures and sprinkle holy water. With each word spoken, the shadows seemed to recede, but the whispering and moaning kept increasing, as if they were reluctant to leave the house.

Suddenly, the floor of the mansion began to shake, and a dark crack opened in the centre of the hall. Evil spirits and hideous creatures emerged from it, released by Isidro's ritual. Horrified, the servant ran into the hall, admitting his mistake and pleading Father Alejandro to stop the invasion of the dark forces.

Father Alejandro urged those present to join forces in a desperate attempt to close the abyss and banish the evil entities. The priest sprinkled holy water over the crack and held a crucifix aloft, while the others prayed. Catalina began to convulse.

In a terrifying climax, the crack slowly began to close, and the evil creatures and spirits were dragged back into the abyss. Finally, with a shuddering cry of defeat, the Shadow of the Abyss disappeared.

With the Shadow of the Abyss and the other evil entities banished, a sepulchral silence fell over the Montenegro mansion. Exhausted but relieved, Father Alejandro, Catalina, Don Esteban and Isidro embraced each other in a gesture of gratitude and victory.

Isidro, aware of his role in the release of the dark forces, knelt before Don Esteban and Catalina, begging their forgiveness and promising to dedicate the rest of his life to making amends for his mistakes. Don Esteban, moved by the servant's remorse and grateful for his sincerity, accepted his apology and allowed him to stay in the mansion.

Father Alejandro, for his part, felt called to carry out a mission to help those who, like Catalina, had been tormented by dark forces. The priest decided to journey the Philippine Islands in search of other souls who needed his help and knowledge to confront the shadows that threatened to destroy their lives.

Catalina and Don Esteban, freed from the terror that had consumed their home, began to rebuild their life together. The young lady, who had lived in anguish for so long, began to regain her happiness and to enjoy the things that life had to offer.

As the years passed, the story of the Shadow of the Abyss and the confrontation at Montenegro Manor became a legend told in the dark and stormy nights.

The mansion, though still imposing, ceased to be a dark and threatening place and became a symbol of hope and renewal for its inhabitants and those who listened to its story.

However, in the depths of the abyss, evil entities waited patiently for the opportunity to return to the world of the living and take revenge on those who had banished them to the depths of darkness. Somehow, the book of rituals that opened the portal had returned to the mansion's library, waiting for someone to read it...

The basement of sighs

Valeria Ortega gazed at the old building she had decided to restore. The stone and brick construction, with its forged iron balconies and arched windows, exuded an air of mystery and grandeur. Located in the centre of Mexico City, the building had a history that Valeria hoped to uncover and preserve in her *boutique* hotel project.

Raúl Elizondo, the owner of the building and descendant of the family that originally built it, met her at the entrance. With a smile, he handed her the keys and wished her success in her project. As Valeria explored the building, she couldn't help but feel a strange presence, as if someone else was watching her.

That night, after inspecting every corner of the building, Valeria decided to take a walk around the district to meet her new neighbours.

On her walk, she met Lupe, a girl who lived next door. With a curious and concerned look in her eyes, Lupe asked Valeria if she had heard about the strange happenings related to the basement of the building.

Intrigued, Valeria listened attentively as Lupe told her stories of voices in the night and objects disappearing without explanation. According to the girl, the basement of the building was known in the neighbourhood as 'El sótano de los suspiros' (The basement of sighs).

She also warned Valeria to be careful, as several previous workers had left the place, terrified by what they had experienced there.

Upon returning to the building, Valeria couldn't help but feel intrigued and scared at the same time. What mysteries did the basement of sighs hide? She decided that the next day she would go down to the basement and start investigating for herself.

Valeria didn't sleep well that night. Lupe's words and stories about the basement of sighs kept her awake.

The next morning, on the Day of the Dead, armed with an ancient lantern and her curiosity, Valeria opened the door leading to the basement. The musty smell and the cold hit her instantly, as if the basement was a world apart from the rest of the building. She carefully descended the stone stairs, illuminating the way with her lantern.

The basement was large and dark, with stone and brick walls showing signs of wear and abandonment. While Valeria explored the place, she noticed that the cold was getting more intense and the air seemed charged with energy.

Suddenly, she felt a blast of cold air that made her skin crawl and she heard an almost inaudible voice, as if someone was trying to communicate with her. Despite the shivers, she decided to keep going.

As she went on, she discovered a hidden corner behind some old boxes and spiderwebs. There she found a door locked with a rusty padlock. Reaching for a hammer, she smashed the lock and opened the door, revealing a small room full of old, dusty objects. Among the objects, she found a diary that seemed to have belonged to Frida, Raúl's great-grandmother.

Valeria decided to take the diary with her and start reading it in search for clues about the strange events of the basement. As she was climbing the stairs to leave, she heard the voice again, this time clearer and almost like a plea. Valeria stopped, feeling a mixture of fear and compassion, and promised herself that she would discover the truth behind the basement of sighs.

She began to read Frida's diary. The yellowed pages and the antique aroma transported her to another era. As she read, Valeria learned about the life of Frida, a passionate and determined woman who lived in the building during the late 19th century.

Frida wrote about her love for music, her family and her husband, Roberto. However, woven into her writings were also tales of sadness and loss. Frida mentioned a daughter named Lourdes, who had died in tragic and mysterious circumstances in the basement of the building. The girl, according to the diary, had been found lifeless in the same hidden room that Valeria had discovered.

As she kept on reading, Valeria felt the connection between her and Frida growing stronger. Frida's words seemed to come alive, and Valeria could hear her voice narrating the stories. In the diary, Frida expressed her conviction that the spirit of Lourdes still haunted the basement, trapped and seeking comfort.

Convinced that she must help Lourdes, Valeria returned to the basement with the diary, a candle and an audio recorder. She intended to obtain *psychophonies*, sounds produced by psychic energy. With the trembling light of the candle illuminating her path, she went back into the hidden room. There, heart pounding, she placed the recorder and began to speak aloud, trying to communicate with the spirit of the girl.

'I'm here to help you, Lourdes,' said Valeria in a soft, trembling voice. 'Your mother, Frida, is worried about you and wants you to find peace.'

As she uttered these words, Valeria felt a presence around her and heard the whisper of a child's voice. Valeria stopped the recording and rewound the tape to listen to what had been recorded. She began to make out words of distress among the sounds. Lourdes, the child trapped in the basement, was trying to communicate with her. Valeria took a deep breath and put aside her fear, ready to help the little girl's spirit.

'What do you need to find peace, Lourdes?' asked Valeria softly. She checked the recorder again. The girl's voice answered with sadness, explaining that there was an object that kept her tied to that place: a small music box that her mother, Frida, had given her shortly before her death.

Valeria, guided by Lourdes' words, looked for the little box among the dusty objects in the hidden room. Finally, she found it, covered in dust and cobwebs, in a corner. The box had a beautiful and detailed design, and when Valeria opened it, a soft, nostalgic melody began to play.

Feeling that she had found what Lourdes needed, Valeria carried the music box to the centre of the room. She placed it on the floor and left it open, allowing the melody to fill the basement. As it did, she felt the energy in the basement change: the cold and sadness that once pervaded her were slowly beginning to dissipate.

As the melody came to an end, Valeria heard a sigh of relief and gratefulness. Lourdes had found the peace she longed for and was ready to leave the basement. Valeria felt a soft, cool breeze envelop her, and knew that Lourdes' spirit was embracing her in gratitude before disappearing.

Exhausted but satisfied, Valeria returned to her apartment with Frida's diary and the music box. She had freed Lourdes and, in doing so, had also freed the basement from the sadness and mystery that surrounded it. Life in the building returned to normal, but Valeria would never forget the experience she shared with Lourdes. After all, the little music box never stopped playing every night, without having to open it...

The enigma of the red moon

In the final epoch of the Reconquest, when the struggle between Moors and Christians was at its peak, a group of brave Christian warriors led by Don Fernando de León advanced through the mountains in search of a Moorish stronghold.

It was the time of the red moon, a rare celestial phenomenon, which hovered in the night sky, covering the land with an ominous mantle of gloom.

Don Fernando, together with his men and his faithful companion Friar Martín de la Vega, set out into the mountains, guided by the Christian spy Alfonso. As they penetrated into the dark landscape, the atmosphere became heavier and more sinister.

They were also accompanied by Hakim, a Moorish doctor who had been captured by Don Fernando's soldiers. Despite being his enemy, Don Fernando decided to free him and allow him to join his group, as he believed in the value of mercy and compassion in times of war.

During the night, the warriors stopped to rest around a campfire. Their faces were partially illuminated by the dancing flames. The crackling of the fire provided an eerie echo as Alfonso began to share his discoveries about the red moon:

'Listen, brothers. I have researched the legend of the red moon in these lands, and what I found is shocking. According to local stories, when the moon turns this sanguine colour, it is a harbinger of misfortune and death.'

'Misfortune and death, you say, Alfonso? We cannot be frightened by superstitions,' said one of the soldiers.

'Tonight,' exclaimed another soldier, 'as we were marching, I felt a strange presence in the forest.'

'If the legends are true,' Alfonso continued, 'we should be prepared to face whatever lurks in the shadows.'

All went silent while uncertainty loomed ominously.

As the night wore on, the echoes of the cries and wails of the souls in pain began to echo through the valley. The group entered a nearby cave in search of shelter, but in doing so, they discovered that the cave was marked with strange and ancient symbols that seemed to be related to the red moon entity.

Don Fernando, determined to unravel the mystery and confront the supernatural entity, urged his men to continue advancing towards the Moorish stronghold. The group of Christian warriors penetrated further into the darkness, unaware that the enigma of the red moon would lead them to face a nightmare.

Once in the valley, they followed the Moors' trail to a stronghold hidden in the mountains. The terrain was becoming increasingly difficult and inaccessible, but the soldiers' determination drove them on.

As they approached the stronghold, the atmosphere became even more sinister. The cries and wails of the souls in pain echoed in the night, mingling with the wind howling through the mountains. Although they tried to stand firm, fear was slowly taking over their hearts.

Once they reached the gates of the bastion, Don Fernando ordered his men to prepare for the assault.

However, the stronghold had been abandoned.

The Moorish physician Hakim, who knew the truth about what the place was, begged Don Fernando to leave the bastion and return to his lands. But Don Fernando, driven by the need to unlock the mystery and protect his people from the supernatural threat, decided to stay and explore the stronghold in search for answers.

They went deeper into the dark bowels of the bastion, finding more and more signs of the presence of the mysterious entity. Friar Martín de la Vega, crucifix in hand, prayed fervently for protection from the evil that stalked them.

Finally, deep inside the stronghold, they discovered an ancient ritual hall, where the Moors had attempted to conjure the red moon entity. Don Fernando and his group of Christian warriors prepared themselves to confront it. As the moon reached its highest point in the sky, it faintly illuminated the interior of the bastion with its bloody glow, announcing that the battle between good and evil was about to begin.

Friar Martin de la Vega, armed with his crucifix and his faith, led the group in prayer, asking for divine protection in the impending battle against the forces of evil. While they recited the sacred words, a powerful and purifying energy began to flow through them, strengthening their souls.

The group set out to confront the entity and a terrifying presence began to materialise in the room. It turned out to be a battalion of wraiths, dead Moorish soldiers whose ghosts continued to fight on red moon nights. The spirits swooped down and attacked them. The Christian warriors fought bravely, with Don Fernando and his men facing the impossible.

Squire Diego Garcia and Alfonso, the spy, tried to protect Friar Martin. The ghosts did not attack Hakim, for they recognised his condition.

The fight was intense and brutal, with the spectres of the red moon showing their supernatural power. Then, Don Fernando decided to use the sword Tizona, the one that once belonged to The Cid Campeador. The spectres saw it and recognised the sword that slew them. With piercing screams, the warrior ghosts disappeared.

When the red moon began to fade over the horizon, Friar Martin concluded his prayers, and a bright, purifying light flooded the room.

Exhausted but victorious, Don Fernando and his companions gathered in the ritual hall. They had successfully confronted the red moon entity and banished it forever.

Although the fight had scarred their bodies and souls, they knew they had protected their people from an unimaginable supernatural threat.

With their mission accomplished, the group left the Moorish stronghold and returned to their homeland. Even though the riddle of the red moon was resolved, the stories of their bravery and sacrifice were told for generations, becoming legends that would live on through the ages.

The cemetery of the living

On the eve of Samaín in 1984, Aleixo was driving his car along a solitary road in the middle of the Galician countryside. The rain was falling heavily, and visibility was very poor. He was anxious to reach his destination, but suddenly, the engine started to fail and the car stopped right in front of an old cemetery.

Unable to repair the car in the pouring rain, Aleixo decided to seek shelter in the cemetery caretaker's gatehouse, perhaps there would be a phone there to call someone.

As he approached, he could see the gravestones on the ground, covered with moss and leaves, and a sombre atmosphere surrounded him.

Gustavo, the cemetery caretaker, opened the door to the gatehouse and greeted him with a friendly smile. The old man offered him a place to sit and something hot to drink while they waited for the rain to stop, since the telephone was not working.

As Aleixo settled in and sipped his hot coffee, Gustavo told him stories about the cemetery and its inhabitants. Aleixo, intrigued by the stories, began to feel a strange connection to the place.

When the rain eased a little, Aleixo decided to take a walk through the cemetery to stretch his legs and explore the area. As he walked, he met Helena, an elegant and mysterious woman who seemed to be waiting for him.

Helena, with an enigmatic gaze, began to talk to Aleixo about the cemetery's past and how each person buried there had a unique and interesting story. Intrigued, Aleixo followed Helena as she guided him among the graves. She introduced him to Carlos, Victoria, Ernesto and Antón, each with their own tale to tell.

As the group of strangers introduced themselves, Aleixo began to sense that something strange was happening. Although everyone seemed friendly and welcoming, there was an air of mystery and fear in the air.

The night progressed, and the characters of the cemetery insisted on Aleixo spending the night there with them, sharing their adventures and experiences. Despite his fears and suspicions, Aleixo became curious and fascinated by these people who seemed to know all the secrets of the cemetery and of life and death itself.

Hoping to discover the truth behind these mysterious visitors of the cemetery, Aleixo decided to stay and explore further, unaware that he was about to face an unimaginable terror.

As the night grew darker and the wind whistled through the gravestones, the mysterious characters of the cemetery began to tell their stories. Aleixo, increasingly intrigued, listened attentively as he immersed himself in the lives of these individuals.

Carlos, a brave and adventurous sailor, spoke of his days at sea and the fierce storms he had faced. His story was full of love, betrayal and the struggle for survival.

Victoria, a young noblewoman, narrated her tragic life, marked by an arranged marriage and a forbidden love that drove her to despair.

Ernesto, a talented doctor, told how his obsession with science and the pursuit of knowledge led him to forbidden experiments that ended in disaster and his own condemnation.

Antón, a humble peasant, described his life of poverty and his insatiable desire for justice and revenge that led him to betrayal.

As the stories unfolded, Aleixo realised that, despite their differences, they all shared a sense of grief and longing for what they had lost. But there was also something else, something he could not identify, that united them all.

When the bells of a nearby church resounded, Aleixo began to feel a shiver running down his spine. Despite his fascination with the stories, he couldn't help but feel a growing fear and a sense that something very bad was about to happen.

The characters of the cemetery seemed increasingly anxious and worried, as if the moment of truth was near. Aleixo, unable to resist the curiosity and the urge to know what was going on, decided to confront his hosts and ask them directly about the mystery surrounding them.

At his insistence, Helena finally revealed the truth they had been hiding: they were all, in fact, ghosts trapped in the cemetery, condemned to relive their stories and regrets forever. With a sense of horror, Aleixo began to understand the implications of his decision to stay in the cemetery that night.

Helena continued her revelation in a trembling voice. The curse of the cemetery affected all those who lay buried there and manifested itself with particular intensity during Samaín. The spirits of the dead were forced to wander the cemetery, desperately searching for someone who would listen to them and perhaps help them find peace.

Aleixo felt a mixture of compassion and fear as he listened to Helena's confession. He looked at the ghosts around him, Carlos with his sad expression, Victoria with her tear-filled eyes, Ernesto with his serious countenance and Antón with his barely contained rage.

Then Helena revealed a more sinister part of the curse: if a visitor spent the whole night in the cemetery during Samaín, their souls would be freed, but the visitor's one would be trapped there forever, condemned to wander and relive his own sorrows and regrets. Panic began to take hold of Aleixo as he realised the trap he had fallen into.

He thought of a way to escape, but the sun's rays of dawn touched his face. His fate was sealed. He was trapped in that graveyard. Now, he was alone.

Whispers in the dark

On a lugubrious evening in late October, Jonathan Hawthorne stood before the rusty iron bars of the gate guarding the entrance to the old Boston mansion he had inherited from a distant, unknown relative. The structure, standing ominously against a bleak landscape, seemed to hold secrets waiting to be discovered. Jonathan's heart pounded with a mixture of fascination and dread as he pushed at the gate, which creaked as if protesting the interruption of its eternal slumber.

The mansion, though neglected and overgrown with ivy, possessed a gothic beauty that attracted Jonathan like a magnet. The gloomy and melancholic atmosphere of the house resembled his own lonely spirit, and the young scholar could not help but feel a strange affinity with his new home.

Once inside the mansion, Jonathan began to explore its dark corners and winding corridors, his feet echoing on the worn wooden floors. As he advanced, he couldn't help but feel that he was being watched by something unseen, something that seemed to be mumbling his name from the shadows.

Late at night, as Jonathan delved into the mysteries of an ancient tome of the occult, a gust of icy wind blew through the open window, causing the candle flames to flicker and murmur. It was then that he heard the whisper for the first time, a barely audible sound that seemed to come from the depths of the mansion:

'Jonathan...'

Intrigued and frightened, Jonathan followed the voice to the basement, where he found a door hidden behind a dusty shelf. Pushing the door with trembling hands, the young scholar discovered a secret room, whose walls were covered with arcane inscriptions and symbols.

Exploring the room, his eyes fell upon an ancient locket, inside which rested a portrait of a hauntingly beautiful woman. As he gazed upon the woman's face, the whispers in the darkness seemed to grow louder and more insistent, as if calling him from beyond.

At that moment, Jonathan was startled to see in the room Elizabeth Sinclair, the mysterious and charming neighbour who lived next door. Elizabeth, who had been drawn to Jonathan's house by its aura of mystery and melancholy, shared the young scholar's interest in the supernatural. Together, they decided to delve into the mansion's hidden secrets and unravel the nature of the whispers in the darkness that seemed to haunt Jonathan.

But someone was observing the young adults join forces to explore the mysteries of the mansion. Reverend Samuel Abbot and the town's inhabitants were following their steps with growing interest.

As the days faded and the nights grew longer and darker, Jonathan and Elizabeth continued their investigation of the whispers in the dark. They spent hours wandering the corridors of the mansion, searching for any trace of their origin and purpose. But with each step they took into the shadows, they felt how darkness enveloped them more and more, like a cold, seductive embrace.

Reverend Abbot, aware of their nocturnal activities, became increasingly concerned. With a growing fear in his heart, the stern Puritan minister began to warn the town's citizens of the dangers of getting involved with the occult, and urged them to avoid any contact with the two young people, whom he considered dangerous and corrupt.

Jonathan and Elizabeth, unaware of the reverend's suspicions and accusations, continued their search for answers. One afternoon, while exploring the basement of the mansion, they discovered a series of old documents and diaries written by Jonathan's late relative. Among the yellowed and dusty pages, they found eerie accounts of dark rites and pacts with unknown entities.

Fascinated and terrified in equal parts, they decided to seek the help of Nathaniel Mortimer, an eccentric old man who lived on the outskirts of town and was rumoured to have knowledge of the region's hidden secrets. Despite the reverend's warnings and the murmurs of disapproval from the townsfolk, the couple visited the old man at his home, a ramshackle, overgrown cottage.

Nathaniel, seeing the concern in his visitors' eyes, agreed to share his knowledge of the whispers in the darkness and the shadows that haunted Jonathan's mansion. He explained that the entity inhabiting the house had been summoned by Jonathan's relative in a desperate attempt to gain forbidden knowledge.

In doing so, however, the relative had unleashed forces beyond his control, sealing his fate and that of the manor. Nathaniel told them that the only way to confront and free the manor from the shadows that haunted it was through an ancient ritual. They had to gather personal items and perform an act of contrition to purify the house and rid it of the evil influence. He also warned them that the ritual would be dangerous and would require courage and determination from all involved parts.

Armed with this new information, Jonathan and Elizabeth returned to the mansion, resolved to confront the supernatural.

But as they penetrated into the depths of the house, the whispering voices become louder and the shadows seemed to grow and twist around them. In the heart of darkness, the couple began to realise that the price for unravelling the secrets of the mansion could be far higher than they had ever imagined.

On the outside, Reverend Abbot and many citizens of Boston, aware of the growing threat emanating from the mansion, gathered in a fearful and angry crowd. With torches in hand and prayers on their lips, they marched towards the mansion, determined to put an end to the darkness that had fallen upon their town.

Swirling shadows and incomprehensible murmurs filled the air as Jonathan and Elizabeth moved deeper into the bowels of the mansion.

As they progressed, the boundaries between reality and fantasy seemed to blur, and the young pair was assailed by visions of unspeakable horrors and nightmares come true.

In one of the visions, they saw a hooded, black-clad figure floating in the air, with hollow eyes that seemed to stare directly into their souls. The figure stretched out its arms towards them as an icy wind filled the room.

Elizabeth saw in a dark room a porcelain girl, with an unsettling face, slowly approaching. With her every step, the room was filled with giggles and laughing children's voices that became increasingly perturbing.

In another vision, they found themselves trapped in a dark, lush forest that seemed to have no end. Trees writhed like snakes, and menacing spectres moved among the branches, mumbling incomprehensible words.

Both saw their loved ones turned into grotesque twisted versions of themselves. Their faces were melting and their hollow eyes were empty, as they begged for help in a distorted language.

In a particularly terrifying vision, they found themselves on the edge of an unfathomable abyss. A howling wind pushed them forward, as if the abyss was calling them. They could hear voices from the depths, promising dark knowledge and unimaginable powers.

Despite the fear that consumed them, they clung to each other and continued their descent into the unfathomable abyss that lurked deep within the mansion. With each step, the power of the shadows and the whispers seemed to grow, and they began to feel their sanity crumble under the weight of unbearable revelations.

Finally, they reached the heart of the abyss, where they discovered an ancient altar covered in arcane symbols and dark stains that looked like dried blood. At that moment, the dark entity that had been whispering in the darkness revealed itself, appearing as a mass of twisted, deformed shadows that seemed to devour the light around it.

Terrified, Jonathan and Elizabeth attempted to perform a banishing ritual, using the knowledge they had acquired from Nathaniel Mortimer and the ancient documents of the manor. But as they spoke the arcane words, the entity unleashed its fury upon them, creating a whirlwind of darkness that threatened to consume them both.

At that crucial moment, the crowd led by Reverend Abbot stormed the mansion, carrying with them the light of torches and the strength of their faith. United in a last desperate effort, Jonathan, Elizabeth and the crowd faced the dark entity, praying and chanting together to drive it from their world.

With a cry of agony and fury, the shadow dissolved into darkness, and the whispering ceased abruptly. Exhausted but triumphant, they all looked at each other in gratitude for having survived the depths of the unfathomable abyss.

Although the threat of the whispers in the dark had been eradicated, Jonathan and Elizabeth would never forget the visions in the heart of the mansion. And though their lives went on, they would always carry with them a reminder of the darkness that had inhabited their home and their souls.

The mansion, once mired in darkness, seemed to have regained some of its former glory, and a glimmer of light returned to its dark corners. The citizens of Boston, though relieved by the banishment of the evil entity, looked with suspicion and distrust at the pair, who had defied the impossible and survived.

Despite the shadows of the past, the young couple found solace in each other, sharing their love for the mysterious and the unknown, as well as the weight of what they had experienced. Together, they restored the mansion and began to seek a new, quieter life, away from the shadows and whispers that had once haunted their days and nights.

However, the darkness had not completely dissipated, and its echoes still resided in the hearts and minds of those who were touched by its embrace. Reverend Abbot, though he led the citizens in their confrontation with the entity, could not escape the unsettling sense that something sinister still lurked in the shadows of the mansion and in the souls of Jonathan and Elizabeth.

Obsessed by his suspicions and fears, the reverend began to watch the couple again, convinced that the darkness would return to claim what was his. Days passed and, consumed by his paranoia, the reverend drifted further away from his faith and his community, until he became a reflection of what he had sworn to fight. Jonathan and Elizabeth, aware of the reverend's vigilance, strove to maintain peace and harmony in their home, trying to prove to their neighbours and to themselves that the darkness had been vanquished.

But deep in their hearts, they both knew that the scars left by the whispers in the dark would never completely disappear.

On a stormy night, as lightnings lit up the sky and thunders shook the foundations of the earth, Reverend Abbot burst into the mansion, convinced that the time had come to confront the darkness he believed still resided in Jonathan and Elizabeth. But in his fury and desperation, the reverend unleashed his own darkness, sparking a confrontation that would change their lives forever.

The mansion seemed to have a life of its own. The paintings on the walls distorted their images and emitted horrifying screams. Lamps flickered on and off, leaving them in darkness for brief moments that seemed eternal. An icy wind picked up in the room, causing the candles to flicker and go out. Spectral shadows twisted and gathered over Reverend Abbot, trying to suffocate his faith.

It was at that moment, amidst the storm and the supernatural confrontation, that Jonathan and Elizabeth realised the truth: the darkness not only resided in the mansion, it was also within themselves.

The secret of the swamp

The full moon was shining in the night sky, illuminating the murky waters of the swamp that stretched outside the small Egyptian village. Khenemet and Senet, two adventurous young girls, hid behind some reeds, peering intently into the forbidden area that had always intrigued the villagers.

It was said that the swamp hid a dark secret connected to the *hatia* Ankhara, the mayor, and whoever dared to enter it would disappear without a trace. However, Khenemet's curiosity led her to seek the truth behind legends, convincing her friend Senet to accompany her.

As they entered the swamp, the girls noticed how the atmosphere became denser and more sinister. The sounds of insects and frogs disappeared abruptly, leaving an eerie silence.

With each step they took, they felt fear creep over them, but their curiosity to discover the secret drove them on.

As they walked, Khenemet remembered the words of her mother, Hathora, who had warned her of the danger lurking in the swamp. Hathora shared with her daughter an ancient legend about a mythical creature that protected the swamp and the secrets it held, but Khenemet always had the feeling that her mother knew something more.

Suddenly, the girls came upon a structure half-hidden in the reeds and mud. It appeared to be an ancient, abandoned temple, with walls covered in hieroglyphs barely visible beneath the dirt and the passage of time. Khenemet and Senet stared at each other, realising they were about to discover something that would change their lives forever.

But before they could get any closer to the temple, a menacing figure emerged from the shadows. Horemheb, the feared warrior of Ankhara, stood between the girls and the temple, his face full of fury.

'You have entered a forbidden place!' Horemheb shouted, his voice echoing through the swamp. 'The *hatia* will not tolerate this insolence!'

Khenemet and Senet, terrified but brave, thought of a way to evade the warrior and continue their search. They agreed to run in different directions, for he could follow only one and the other one would have a chance to enter.

But in that instant, a terrifying howl echoed through the air, causing everyone present to shudder in fear. Something was stirring in the depths of the swamp, and soon the truth behind the dark secret that had remained hidden for years would be revealed.

The bloodcurdling howl made Horemheb, Khenemet and Senet stop in their tracks. The swamp seemed to come alive as the shadows stirred and the water bubbled around them.

Without missing a beat, Khenemet took advantage of the warrior's distraction and, grabbing Senet by the hand, she ran towards the temple.

They entered the temple and discovered that the walls were covered with hieroglyphs that told a story of betrayal and curse. Khenemet, who learned to read hieroglyphs from Sobekhotep, the old scholar, translated the story. The legend spoke of a dark pact between the *hatia* Ankhara and the swamp creature, Ammit, to maintain the power in the village in exchange for fresh meat for the beast.... human sacrifices!

Frightened but determined to stop this atrocity, Khenemet and Senet emerged from the temple, only to come face to face with the terrifying swamp creature. Ammit, with his wolf head, crocodile body and huge clawed hands, towered over them, his gaze piercing and his jaws open in a terrifying roar.

But before Ammit could attack the girls, a mysterious force seemed to stop the creature in place. The girls watched in amazement as Khenemet's necklace, an heirloom that had belonged to their mother, began to glow with an intense light, immobilising Ammit and allowing them to escape.

With the creature momentarily detained, the two friends ran back to the village, hoping to warn the villagers and stop the sinister pact between the *hatia* and the beast. Before they could reached it, they ran into Neferu, the priest and advisor to the mayor.

'I know what you have discovered,' said Neferu with a sly smile. 'But I will not allow you to ruin my plans. The *hatia* and I have worked hard to maintain control, and I will not allow two petty girls to destroy it.'

The girls kept running, knowing now that they had to face the priest and the *hatia* to stop the sinister pact and free their people from the curse. They sought the help of the ancient scholar Sobekhotep. He revealed to them that the necklace of Khenemet was an ancient amulet of protection, which had the power to stop the ancient beasts.

With this information in mind, Khenemet and Senet devised a plan to infiltrate the *hatia*'s house and confront him, exposing the truth about the pact and the betrayal he had committed against his people. With the help of some brave villagers, the girls managed to force their way into the house.

Once inside, they sought out Ankhara, who was surrounded by advisors, including Neferu. Khenemet and Senet approached, mustering the courage to confront the ruler.

'Hatia Ankhara!' shouted Khenemet. 'We come to expose the truth about the dark pact you have made with the swamp creature, Ammit. You have betrayed your people and caused suffering and death in the name of power!'

Ankhara looked at the girls with surprise, as Neferu tried to persuade the *hatia to* execute them for treason. Neferu seemed to exert a mysterious control over Ankhara.

Khenemet, displaying the glowing necklace, challenged Neferu and Ankhara to deny the truth that they had discovered. At that moment, the house began to shake, and the doors burst open, revealing Ammit. The creature stepped into the house, its terrifying presence filling the room.

The villagers, who followed Khenemet and Senet to the mayor's house, watched as the creature approached the *hatia* and the priest, ready to fulfil its part of the pact and receive their sacrifice. In an act of courage and determination, Khenemet raised the amulet, which glowed brighter than ever, and pointed it at Ammit.

The creature stood still, and the villagers took advantage of this opportunity to attack it with their farming tools. Together they tore the beast to pieces, avenging the death of their missing relatives.

With Ammit defeated and the dark pact broken, the atmosphere in the house switched from terror to relief. The *hatia* Ankhara, aware of the magnitude of his betrayal and the suffering he had caused, knelt before Khenemet and Senet, asking their forgiveness for his actions.

'I owe you everything,' confessed Ankhara. 'You saved our people from the curse I brought upon myself under the influence of Neferu. I vow that from this day forward, I will rule with justice and wisdom, and I will never allow ambition and power to darken my judgement again.'

Neferu, the priest who devised the pact with the beast, attempted to escape justice, but was captured by Horemheb and other warriors loyal to the *hatia*. Neferu was brought before Ankhara, who ordered him to be mummified alive, ensuring that he could never again harm his people.

Ankhara, grateful for the lesson Khenemet and Senet had taught him, appointed Sobekhotep as his new advisor and pledged to rule justly and fairly. The girls, for their part, returned to their daily lives in the village, though they never forgot the adventure that had brought them face to face with dark creatures and forces.

The swamp, once a place of terror and mystery, was now a quiet place. However, occasionally you could still hear the water bubbling.

The abandoned asylum

Léa Moreau, a young journalist, had heard rumours about an old abandoned asylum on the outskirts of Paris. Stories of inhuman experiments, mysterious disappearances and paranormal phenomena had intrigued her.

Determined to uncover the truth, Léa and her partner Émile Dupont, a talented photographer with a mysterious past, set out to investigate the place.

They made their way to the asylum on a cloudy and gloomy day. As they approached the building, the atmosphere became increasingly stranger. The asylum, in ruins and covered with vines, seemed to be watching them with its broken and worn-out windows.

Léa and Émile cautiously entered the building, equipped with torches and cameras. The interior of the asylum was in a state of total abandonment, with debris and remnants of medical equipment strewn everywhere. At every step they felt they were being watched by invisible eyes.

In one of the rooms, they found an old archive covered in dust and mould. Léa leafed through the patients' files, finding one that caught her eye: Isabelle, a young woman who had mysteriously disappeared shortly before the asylum closed. Resolved to find out what had happened to Isabelle, they searched the place for more clues.

While exploring the outside of the asylum, Léa and Émile met Madame Leclerc, an elderly woman who lived nearby and claimed to have witnessed strange phenomena there, like the sight of silhouettes and the sounds of wailing. Despite her frail appearance, Madame Leclerc proved to be a valuable source of information. She told them about Dr. Charles Gauthier and Dr. François Delacroix, two psychiatrists who had worked at the asylum and who, according to rumour, were involved in dark and questionable experiments on the patients.

Intrigued and alarmed by Madame Leclerc's stories, they decided to visit Dr. Gauthier, who still lived in the city, with the hope of getting answers about the asylum and its terrible secrets.

However, as they prepared to leave the place, an unseen presence made them feel like they were not alone. The lights of their torches began to flicker, and suddenly, a whispering voice filled the air, saying:

'Don't forget me.... Isabelle... Don't forget me...'

Léa and Émile looked at each other, their hearts pounding. They knew they were about to plunge into a mystery much deeper and more terrifying than they had ever imagined. But their inquisitive minds wanted to know the truth.

After their chilling encounter in the asylum, Léa and Émile tracked down Dr. Charles Gauthier's address and went to his home in Paris. The house was in a secluded area, surrounded by trees and shadows that seemed to hide secrets in every corner.

Arriving at the house, the couple could not help but feel some trepidation. Léa summoned her courage and knocked on the door, which was answered by Dr. Gauthier himself. The man, now in his golden years, had a penetrating gaze and a presence that conveyed a mixture of authority and mystery.

With diplomacy, Léa explained to the doctor that they were investigating the abandoned asylum and wanted to ask him some questions. Dr. Gauthier, at first reluctant, ended up inviting them into his study, where he offered them *café crème* while they talked.

He told them about his work at the asylum and his collaboration with Dr. François Delacroix, but avoided speaking about the inhuman experiments that Madame Leclerc had told them about. Léa skilfully brought up the case of Isabelle, the missing patient.

The doctor seemed uncomfortable at the mention of Isabelle, but eventually revealed that she had been subjected to an experimental and dangerous treatment, led by Dr. Delacroix. According to Gauthier, Isabelle had disappeared during one of the treatment sessions, and was never heard from again.

When Léa and Émile pressed for more details, Dr. Gauthier became defensive and asked them to leave his house. Before going, Léa managed to take a photo of Isabelle's file that the doctor had in his study. As they left the mansion, they both sensed that there was much more to Isabelle's story than Dr. Gauthier had revealed.

That same evening, while Léa and Émile were reviewing the information they had gathered, they received a call from Captain Laurent Dubois, a police officer who learned of their investigation. Although initially sceptical, the captain informed them that he had found Dr. Delacroix's body in the abandoned asylum some years ago, but the case was never solved.

With this new information, Léa and Émile decided to return to the asylum to search for more clues about Isabelle's disappearance and the mysterious death of Dr. Delacroix. But, they could not imagine the horrors that awaited them in the depths of that forgotten place.

This time, they returned accompanied by Captain Laurent Dubois, who had begun to believe the couple's claims about the asylum and its murky secrets. As they entered the building, the group sensed once again the unsettling presence that seemed to lurk in the shadows. However, they didn't let fear stop them and continued onward, exploring areas they had not visited before.

In a concealed room in the basement, they discovered an old laboratory where Dr. Delacroix had conducted his experiments. Among the flasks and rusted medical instruments, they found documents detailing the terrible treatments that Isabelle and other patients had been subjected to in the name of science:

- Electroconvulsive therapy: sessions were conducted where electric shocks were applied to patients in order to calm their mental disorders. These practices often left patients traumatised and with permanent brain damage.

- Confinement therapy: patients were locked in small dark cells for days or even weeks. The extreme isolation and lack of stimulation often aggravated their mental conditions.

- Hydrotherapy: patients were immersed in baths of hot or cold water for long periods of time. This therapy was believed to have healing properties, but in reality, it was a form of torture and mistreatment.

- Lobotomy: lobotomies were performed on patients, a surgery that involved the removal or destruction of parts of the brain. This practice often left patients with severe disabilities and debilitating side effects.

- Straitjackets: patients were immobilised in straitjackets, which prevented them from moving and often caused extreme pain and discomfort.

- Altered Feeding: some patients were subjected to extremely restrictive diets or force-fed as part of their treatments.

- Insulin therapy: insulin was administered to patients in dangerously high doses, often resulting in hypoglycaemia and convulsions.

As they explored the lab, Léa, Émile and Captain Dubois began to hear distant voices and moans. Following the sounds, they came to a series of hidden cells in which the most troublesome patients had been locked up. Horrified, they realised that some of the patients had died in their cells, abandoned and forgotten by the asylum staff.

Among the cells, they found one that had been occupied by Isabelle. The young woman's spirit appeared before them, revealing her tragic fate. She told them how Dr. Delacroix had subjected her to ruthless experiments, which drove her to the brink of madness and death.

Isabelle also revealed that the vengeful spirit of Dr. Delacroix still haunted the asylum, seeking to punish those who had unravelled his secrets.

'Dr. Delacroix fears the truth and the light,' she told them.

Before disappearing, Isabelle warned them to be careful, for the doctor's ghost would not rest until his revenge was complete.

With hearts full of fear, sadness and determination, the three vowed to bring justice for Isabelle and the other patients who had suffered in the asylum. But first, they would have to face the furious spirit of Dr. Delacroix and free the place from its dark curse.

The three of them went into the depths of the asylum in search of the spirit of Dr. Delacroix. With each step, the whispers and moans of the spirits trapped in the place grew louder, reminding them of the suffering that occurred there.

Eventually, the group reached an old operating room where Dr. Delacroix had conducted his most terrible experiments. Upon entering the room, they sensed an evil presence watching them from the shadows. Suddenly, the spirit of Dr. Delacroix appeared before them, his face twisted with rage and madness.

The doctor's ghost accused the three of interfering with his experiments and attempting to tarnish his legacy. He swore he would make them suffer like his patients had suffered. However, the group stood their ground, confronting the ghost and demanding him to release the spirits of the patients he had tortured.

Dr. Delacroix, in his fury, unleashed a series of paranormal phenomena in the asylum. Objects flew through the air, doors slammed shut and shadows twisted and morphed into horrific visions. Léa and the others struggled to hold their ground as the asylum seemed to come alive around them.

That was when Léa remembered Isabelle's words: 'Dr. Delacroix fears the truth and the light.' Convinced that truth was her most powerful weapon, Léa faced the spirit and began to recite aloud the names of all the patients who had suffered at the doctor's hands. With each name, the spirit of Dr. Delacroix weakened, while the spirits of the patients began to break free of their bonds.

As Léa spoke the last name, Dr. Delacroix's spirit stirred and collapsed, disappearing in a burst of intense light. The asylum, once filled with suffering and evil, became silent and still. The spirits of the patients, now free, appeared before Léa, Émile and Captain Dubois before disappearing in peace.

Exhausted but satisfied about freeing the trapped spirits, the group left the asylum. Although the scars of the past could never be completely erased, they succeeded in bringing justice and peace to the souls who had suffered there.

Léa and Émile decided it was necessary to ensure that Dr. Delacroix's legacy would not be forgotten, but would stand as a warning so that such atrocities would never be repeated.

With the help of Captain Dubois and his contacts in the police, they gathered all the evidence they had found in the asylum and presented it to the authorities. Although Dr. Delacroix had been dead for years, the story of cruelty and evil that Léa published became a topic of debate in Paris and across the country. Society began demanding more research into the treatments of mentally ill people and exacting accountability.

But many also began visiting the asylum, in search of mystery. There are those who claim to hear and see strange things in the corridors of the building still.

The stairway to hell

Samuel Miller had always been considered a peculiar young man in his Pennsylvanian Amish community. From a young age, he had shown a fascination with the supernatural and the unknown, something that often led to disapproval from his family and neighbours. But Samuel couldn't help but feel a special connection to that enigmatic world that lay beyond his quiet life in the community.

One day, while Samuel was working in the fields, he overheard the adults talking about the disappearance of Ruth Fisher, a ten-year-old girl who had gone missing in the nearby forest. Samuel felt a shiver as he remembered the stories his grandfather told him about the stairway to hell, a local legend that told of a hidden stairway in the forest that led directly to the underworld. According to the stories, those who found the staircase were tempted by dark forces to descend it and they never returned.

In order to discover the truth behind Ruth's disappearance and whether it was connected to the stairway to hell, Samuel asked his friend Rebecca Yoder to join him in his search. Together, they began to secretly investigate, going through old documents and books that had been stored in the community library.

That was when Samuel and Rebecca found an old diary belonging to Elias Schwartz, an elder in the community who had lived there for decades. The journal contained accounts of strange occurrences and sightings in the forest, including mentions of the stairway to hell. Hoping that Elias could shed some light on the mystery, the two friends decided to talk to him.

At first, Elias was reluctant to talk about the staircase, insisting that it was only a legend and had nothing to do with Ruth's disappearance. But Samuel and Rebecca were not to be dissuaded, and in time they got the old man to reveal a dark secret: Elias had seen the stairway to hell with his own eyes many years ago and had witnessed how an evil force spirited away a friend of his who had dared to descend it.

Despite being shocked, they wanted to find Ruth and stop the threat to their community. Samuel and Rebecca embarked on a dangerous mission to locate the stairway to hell and confront the dark forces guarding it. They began their search in the heart of the forest.

For days they searched tirelessly for the stairway to hell, following ancient maps and clues they had discovered in Elias's journal. As they progressed, they began to notice that the animals in the forest seemed to avoid a certain area, as if they knew something evil laid there.

Finally, after almost a week of search, the couple found what they were looking for: a moss-covered stone staircase that seemed to rise from the earth itself.

Even though it apparently had only a few steps, they could both feel the dark energy emanating from it, and there was no doubt in their minds that this was the stairway to hell that Elias had spoken of.

Samuel and Rebecca decided that, before confronting the malevolent forces guarding the staircase, they needed more information and possibly help. They recalled the stories of Hezekiah Stoltzfus, an enigmatic Amish man who lived in isolation from the rest of the community and was rumoured to have knowledge of black magic and the dark arts. While they were concerned about involving someone with such knowledge, they knew they needed all the help they could get.

Cautiously, Samuel and Rebecca approached Hezekiah's house, where they found him sitting on his porch, as if waiting for them. He asked them why they came, and Samuel explained his discovery of the stairway to hell and Ruth's disappearance. Hezekiah listened attentively and told them that he knew how to deal with the dark forces guarding the staircase, but they would have to follow his instructions to the letter.

The young ones agreed, willing to do whatever it took to achieve their purpose. Hezekiah taught them an ancient ritual that he believed would protect them from the demonic entities guarding the stairway to hell. With Hezekiah's help, Samuel and Rebecca prepared to face the darkness, unaware that their greatest test was yet to come.

Together they returned to the place where the stairway to hell was located, ready to confront the unknown. Following Hezekiah's instructions, they began to perform the ancient ritual he had taught them, lighting candles and reciting words in a language none of them understood.

As they performed the ritual, the atmosphere around the staircase began to shift. The night grew even darker, and the air was filled with an unearthly chill that made their skin crawl. Then, before them, a terrifying figure emerged: the Guardian of Hell, a demonic entity with fiery eyes and an evil smile.

The Guardian taunted the young ones, asking them why they had come to confront him. Samuel, mustering his courage, told him they had come to save Ruth and end the threat he posed to their community. The Guardian laughed and told them:

'I will only release the child if one of you takes her place in hell.'

The three Amish looked at each other in horror, knowing they could not abandon Ruth to her fate.

Hezekiah, who lived a solitary life and was full of regrets due to his dealings with black magic, decided to sacrifice himself. He told Samuel and Rebecca that they were young and had their whole lives ahead of them, while he had no one who would miss him. Reluctantly, Samuel and Rebecca accepted Hezekiah's sacrifice, even though it broke their hearts to see him go.

The Guardian accepted the deal and released Ruth, who appeared on the stairs, frightened but unharmed. Hezekiah bade farewell to Samuel and Rebecca and bravely began to descend the staircase into hell as the Guardian followed close behind.

Samuel, Rebecca and Ruth set course back to their community, but then Ruth's face began to change.

It was not her, but a demon from hell, who grabbed the frightened youths. The pair tried to break free but could not and was dragged into the staircase. Samuel and Rebecca's screams echoed through the forest. They were never heard from again. Nor they searched for them.

The cursed ship

The sun was beginning to set on the African coast when the dreaded pirate ship, commanded by Captain William 'Sinister' Hawkins, approached a small fishing village. The crew was eager to plunder and capture slaves, while Captain Hawkins and his first mate, Thomas 'Hook' Blackwell, planned the attack.

The pirates disembarked in the village, where they caused panic among the inhabitants. The population was unable to defend itself against the pirates' brutality.

While the evil plunderers mercilessly slaughtered and captured the young and strong to sell them into slavery, an old woman, wrinkled and hunched, watched from a distance. She was known in the village for her knowledge of the ancient mystic arts.

The pirates razed the village to the ground and returned to the ship with their booty, the captured slaves, including Kofi and Yara, two brave youths who did not let themselves be tied up easily.

Then, the old woman approached and searched the ruins for objects of the pirates. Shreds of clothing, a sword stuck in the wood, blood, and whatever else she could find. Using her knowledge of black magic and voodoo, she cast a curse on the ship and its crew that echoed through the air, and the sky darkened as if nature itself was angered.

While the pirate ship sailed away from the coast, the old woman watched as a dark storm cloud began to follow it. Her eyes shone with a mixture of sadness and satisfaction, knowing that the curse she had cast was her only act of resistance and that the pirates would pay for their atrocities.

On the ship, the pirates were celebrating their victory, unaware that they were doomed by the old woman's curse. Darkness loomed over them, and the beginning of their nightmare was about to begin.

As the pirate ship sailed out to sea, the captured slaves were forced to work in the holds under inhumane conditions. Despite their fear and desperation, Kofi and Yara did not give up hope of finding a chance to escape.

The pirates, however, were busy celebrating their plunder and paid little attention to their prisoners. But as days passed, they began to notice strange little incidents aboard the ship. Some of them swore seeing dark shadows moving across the deck at night, while others spoke of strange nightmares that haunted them.

The captain and his first officer tried to maintain order, but the crew became increasingly restless and superstitious. Fear started to grip everyone as incidents became more frequent and frightening.

It was then that the first fatal accident occurred. One of the pirates, while climbing the mast to adjust the sails, fell into the sea and disappeared into the depths without a trace. The others watched in horror.

As days went by, more pirates died in strange circumstances. Some were lost in the vastness of the ocean, while others were found dead in their cabins with no signs of violence. Panic broke out among the crew, and tensions rose aboard the cursed ship.

Kofi and Yara observed the events from the hold. They began to plan their escape, knowing that the chaos and fear among the pirates could be their chance to break free from their chains and return home.

The crew of the cursed ship continued to dwindle, striking terror into the hearts of the remaining pirates. Captain Hawkins and Blackwell were starting to lose control, it was evident that the old woman's curse was decimating their men.

One night, while the pirates were on deck discussing their fate, Kofi and Yara took advantage of the situation and organised a rebellion among the slaves. United in their desire for vengeance and freedom, the captives rose up against their captors, using the chains that bound them as makeshift weapons.

The battle was fierce, but fear and desperation had weakened the pirates, who were outnumbered and defeated by the slaves. Captain Hawkins and Blackwell were chained and locked in the hold, while Kofi, Yara and the other freed slaves took control of the ship.

Regardless, the curse still lurked, and the vengeful spirits of the dead pirates still seemed to roam around the ship. Kofi and Yara knew they had to get rid of the cursed ship before anything could happened to them and their freed comrades.

One day, while sailing aimlessly, they spotted a group of fishing boats in the distance. They decided to approach and ask for help, hoping to find in these seamen a solution to their terrible situation. The boats belonged to fishermen from the Canary Islands, who listened in astonishment to the story of the youths and their companions.

The Canarian fishermen, moved by their terrible story, decided to help them free themselves from the cursed boat. One of the fishermen, a wise and kind-hearted man named Jesus, suggested that perhaps the old African woman could lift the curse if justice was done.

Following his advice, Kofi and Yara decided to take Hawkins and Blackwell before the old woman and put them on trial for their crimes. With the help of the fishermen, they sailed back to the African village, where they met the old woman and told her everything that happened since their departure.

The old woman agreed to lift the curse, but only if Hawkins and Blackwell paid for their crimes.

The villagers hanged the pirates and devoured their corpses that night, while the old woman lit a bonfire and placed offerings of herbs, a monkey's head and the pirates' objects. Then she chanted ancient litanies and prayers to lift the ship's curse. The vengeful spirits of the pirates were dragged into the underworld, and the cursed ship was freed from the darkness that had consumed it.

The mansion of nightmares

Rain was pouring down torrentially on the English countryside while the Somerset family approached their newly acquired mansion in their carriage. Lady Elizabeth, anxious to arrive, was watching through the windows as the imposing mansion loomed over the horizon. Her children, Charles and Amelia, were uneasy at the thought of moving into an unfamiliar house.

Arriving at the mansion, they were greeted by Mr. Hopkins, the butler, and Mrs. Whitmore, the housekeeper. Both welcomed them to their new home and assured them that the mansion had been prepared for their arrival, despite the short notice.

The following evening, the family had invited the high society of the county to dinner.

As they were all waiting for the exquisite food being prepared by the servants, Lord William told them in high spirits the reason why he was able to acquire the manor at such a good price. He shared the story of the manor and of Lady Rose, the former owner, whose death in mysterious circumstances had left the house empty for years.

Amelia, the youngest, could not help but shudder when she heard the tragic story.

After a sumptuous dinner and a wonderful evening, the guests departed.

As the night wore on, the Somersets began to notice strange details in the house: the sound of footsteps in the empty corridors, an almost inaudible whisper, and the echo of distant weeping. They tried to shrug it off, attributing it to the age of the mansion and their imaginations.

Over the next few days, the mansion began to show its true character. Shadows came to life in dark corners, and mirrors seemed to reflect figures that were not there.

After a week, Mr. Hopkins recommended to Lord William to write to Madame Kardec, a famous French medium, to visit the mansion with her spiritualist associates and help them understand and deal with the strange occurrences. The family hoped that her arrival would shed light on the mysteries of the mansion.

The days passed with increasing tension. The Somersets tried to adjust to their new home, but strange occurrences continued to terrify the family. Lady Elizabeth found displaced objects in her room, while Charles swore seeing a woman walking the corridors.

Amelia, the one most affected by the paranormal phenomena, begun to have nightmares in which a voice urged her to explore the darkest corners of the mansion. On one occasion, she awoke in the middle of the night and, following the voice, made her way to the abandoned greenhouse. There, she found an antique porcelain doll that seemed to speak her name.

While the family was gathered in the living room, they heard shouting and banging coming from upstairs. Lord William, closely followed by Charles, rushed upstairs to discover the source of the commotion. On arriving at Amelia's room, they found the young girl collapsed on the floor, surrounded by floating objects.

It was clear that the goings-on in the mansion were powerful and terrifying.

On one of her walk's trough the mansion, Amelia discovered a secret passage behind a bookshelf in the library. This passageway led to a hidden room, filled with spiritualist objects and antiques. In the centre of the room, there was an altar covered with black candles and a leather-bound book, a sort of summoning manual.

As she studied the contents of the book, Amelia began to suspect that the mansion had been the scene of occult practices in the past, and that perhaps some evil entity had been invoked and had not been properly banished.

For days the Somersets were tormented by visions and nightmares. One night, Lady Elizabeth found Amelia in the garden, under the moonlight, speaking in a strange and incomprehensible language. She and Charles managed to get her back to the mansion and make sure she was safe, but they could not help but wonder if the girl was being possessed by the entity that haunted the house.

On Halloween night, Madame Kardec and her associates arrived at the Somerset mansion. Family and guests gathered in the main hall, where the medium would conduct the séance. The atmosphere was charged with anticipation and dread as the woman sat at a carved wooden table, lit only by flickering candles.

Madame Kardec, a young woman with a mysterious look in her eyes, began to invoke the spirits in a low, solemn voice. She asked those present to hold hands and concentrate on their deceased loved ones. The mansion was completely silent, only the creaking of the old building could be heard.

The medium started babbling incomprehensible words in a strange language as her hands trembled on the table. Suddenly, a cold wind swept through the room, blowing out the candles. The guests shivered as their eyes became accustomed to the darkness.

Then, something incredible happened. A strange, white, vaporous substance began to gush out of Madame Kardec's mouth. Those present recoiled in horror as they watched the ectoplasm flow like a river from the medium's mouth and accumulate on the table. It seemed as if the spirits were trying to manifest through her.

The medium, her face pale and her eyes glazed over, continued to mumble under her breath as the ectoplasm continued to flow. Vague shapes and shadows seemed to take form within the substance. Guests watched in awe and fear as the spirits attempted to communicate.

The ectoplasm stirred frantically, and the atmosphere in the room became increasingly frightening. It was as if the spirits were desperately trying to convey a message.

Then the séance reached its climax when a spectral figure emerged from the ectoplasm, a tormented spirit that had been trapped in the mansion for years. It was Lady Rose. She screamed with immeasurable anguish before vanishing into darkness.

The table shook and the terrified guests broke the chain of hands. The candles lit again on their own, and Madame Kardec fell to the floor, exhausted with a mouthful of blood.

The Somerset mansion was filled with an eerie silence, broken only by the agitated breathing of the frightened people present. Madame Kardec's associates decided to take her to a hospital.

After the terrifying séance, everyone left. The family fled the house in panic. They packed up their essentials and moved to a hotel in town. Mr. Hopkins and Mrs. Whitmore stayed there, watching them leave. The servants were not surprised by anything that happened.

The clock that stopped time

Breda, Netherlands, 1625. The Tercios de Flandes, under the command of Captain Diego Serrano, arrived in the city to reinforce the fight against the Dutch resistance led by the Count of Nassau. The fighting had been intense and arduous, but the Spanish soldiers, seasoned in thousands of battles, held out hope of victory.

One night, while the men were recovering in a local tavern, the young soldier Pedro Velázquez heard a disturbing story about a cursed clock created by the master clockmaker Guillermo van Dijk. According to legend, the clock had the power to stop time and alter the course of history.

Pedro shared the information with his comrades, and though they laughed at first, Lieutenant Francisco de Cárdenas could not help but fell a growing curiosity.

He decided to investigate the matter and went to the master clockmaker's house. When he arrived, he found the house silent and gloomy.

Upon entering, he discovered the lifeless body of the clockmaker, with a terrified expression on his face. On the table, there was a strange, ancient-looking clock, which seemed to have stopped at a specific time.

Francisco decided to take it with him, but as he did, he sensed a dark and frightening presence around him. Nevertheless, he chose to ignore it and returned to the tavern to show it to his companions.

Captain Diego Serrano, seeing the clock, ordered his men to be cautious, for something gave him a bad feeling. That same night, strange events began to happen in the Tercios' camp. Some soldiers swore seeing shadows moving among the tents and heard unintelligible whispers.

Meanwhile, in the city, the mysterious Inés de Herrera, a young woman known for her predictive abilities, had a terrifying vision. In her dream, the clock that stopped time released a supernatural entity that unleashed chaos and destruction in Breda. She decided to approach the camp of the Tercios to warn them of the impending danger. On arriving, she was met by Captain Serrano and told him about her vision.

The captain, concerned for the safety of his men and the city, decided to confront the threat and put an end to the cursed clock. But what they didn't know was that the Count of Nassau had been watching them and planned to use the clock's power for his own benefit.

The Count sent a spy to the camp who stealthily managed to get hold of the clock. The next day, the camp was attacked by the Count of Nassau's forces.

The Tercios defended bravely, but the enemy soldiers moved with astonishing speed, as if time was different for them. The clock was capable of speeding up and slowing down time at the whim of its owner.

Captain Serrano and his men managed to repulse the enemy attack, but at a high cost. Many of the Tercios brave soldiers had fallen in the battle, and the camp was in ruins. The good news was that, in the heat of battle, the Count lost the clock, which was back in Spanish hands.

Inés, Pedro and Francisco tried to keep the clock out of enemy's reach. They entered the nearby forest, but were soon pursued by Nassau's forces.

During the chase, Inés revealed that she was a descendant of an ancient line of witches and that she knew of an ancient sacred well deep in the forest. There, according to her, the clock would be protected by the forces of nature and would be almost impossible to find.

Desperate, but still determined to protect the clock and the city of Breda, they set out in search of the sacred well. Together, they entered the dark and mysterious forest.

The Count of Nassau, furious at his failure, vowed to find the clock and unleash his power on Breda and the Tercios. He would not give up.

The survivors of the Tercios, led by Captain Serrano, continued moving deeper into the thick forest, guided by Inés' knowledge. The stories and legends about the sacred well had been passed down from generation to generation in her family, and now it was her responsibility to protect the cursed clock.

As they went on, Inés shared with them more about her legacy and the dark forces that lurked in the shadows. According to her, the clock was a relic of great power, created by a sorcerer from time immemorial, which had fallen into the wrong hands throughout history, causing havoc and misery.

The search for the sacred well got even more complicated when the group began to experience strange occurrences. They heard voices in the shadows, sensed evil presences watching them, drawn by the power of the clock.

One night, while camping near an old abandoned village, they were attacked by a number of spirits with skeletal bodies.

Inés managed to conjure a spell of fire that drove the spirits away, but they had already inflicted some casualties on the Tercios.

Finally, after days of walking and confrontations with supernatural forces, they reached the sacred well. The place was surrounded by ancient trees and seemed to emanate a special energy, which even the roughest soldiers could feel.

But, there was no time to celebrate. The Count of Nassau and his forces were not far away, and they had to find a way to protect the clock and keep it out of his reach.

Inés suggested to perform an ancestral incantation that, according to her family's legends, could seal the clock and its evil powers in the sacred well forever. But the spell required sacrifices and the cooperation of all present. Despite their doubts, they agreed to participate in the ceremony.

Thus, under the full moon and surrounded by the magic of the sacred well, the Spanish soldiers and Inés began the arduous task. The atmosphere around the well became even more sombre and sinister. Inés began to recite the incantation and the members of the Tercios joined in a circle around the well, holding the clock in their hands.

Suddenly, the sky darkened, and a thunder and lightning storm burst overhead. The soldiers struggled to maintain their composure, but fear and uncertainty began to grip their hearts.

As the spell progressed, Inés revealed the truth behind the sacrifice needed to seal the clock in the sacred well: one of them had to give his life willingly for the spell to work.

The soldiers, shocked and horrified, looked at each other, unable to decide who should do it. Pedro, seeing the fear in the eyes of his comrades, stepped forward and offered himself.

At the climax of the incantation, Pedro, with the clock in his hand, threw himself into the well while Inés recited the last words of the spell. A flash of bright light and a ripple of energy shook the area, and the clock disappeared into the depths of the well.

When the storm subsided, the group mourned the loss of Pedro and thanked Inés for helping them accomplish their mission. Thanks to their bravery, the Count of Nassau was soon defeated.

The castle of the souls

Don Rodrigo's castle stood majestically atop a rocky hill, surrounded by a thick forest that seemed to hold its secrets. Halloween was approaching and Don Rodrigo had organised a costume party in his mysterious home for his friends and high society acquaintances.

Doña Judith, a young and beautiful aristocrat, arrived at the castle with great anticipation, for she had never been to a Halloween party in such an interesting place. As she crossed the drawbridge, she felt a strange energy emanating from the old stones of the castle.

Once inside, the guests were delighted with music, food and drinks in abundance. The atmosphere was one of joy and fun, with all attendees wearing elaborate costumes.

Doña Judith, wearing a golden Venetian mask that revealed her eyes, could not help but be curious about Don Rodrigo, who wore a large hat with exotic animal feathers.

The night progressed and the Count of Valdemar, a vain and arrogant knight, challenged other guests to tell stories of terror and mystery. That was when the Marquise of Linares, an enigmatic woman in a black lace mask, told the story of the spirits that inhabited the castle.

All listened attentively to the legend of how those who had died in the castle centuries ago now wandered its corridors like spectres, trapped between life and death.

Doña Judith looked at Don Rodrigo, but he was unmoved by the story.

When the party was at its peak, Friar Juan, a monk who lived near the castle, burst into the hall with a warning. He implored them to leave the place before midnight, for the curse on the castle would be unleashed that night. The guests, incredulous and somewhat scared, ignored the monk and continued their festivities.

As midnight approached, the atmosphere in the castle began to change. Laughter turned to murmurs and the guests began to sense an unsettling presence. Don Rodrigo, smiling mysteriously, announced it was time to retire to their rooms.

Doña Judith, intrigued by the events of the night and eager to discover the truth, could not imagine the terrors that awaited her in the shadows of the castle of the souls.

As the guests retired to their respective rooms, a sense of dread and anticipation came over them. The echo of footsteps in the dark corridors seemed to echo in their heads, and the shadows cast by the candles created strange figures on the walls. Friar Juan's warning still echoed in their thoughts.

Doña Judith found herself in a luxurious but gloomy room, decorated with old portraits of Don Rodrigo's ancestors. Her eyes could not help but stray to one portrait in particular, a stern-looking woman who seemed to be watching her from the canvas. As she approached the window, Doña Judith noticed a shadow gliding across the courtyard. Curious, she decided to follow the mysterious figure.

Meanwhile, the Count of Valdemar, who did not believe in stories of curses and ghosts, mocked the other guests for their fear.

He decided to walk through the castle to prove that there was nothing to be afraid of, but in his arrogance, he failed to see the shadows that followed him along the corridors.

In her search for the mysterious shadow, Doña Judith wandered into the dark corridors of the castle. Arriving at a spiral staircase, she found it disappearing into what appeared to be a secret passageway. Bravely, she followed the figure into a hidden chamber.

The room was filled with ancient and mysterious objects. In the centre, there was an altar covered in dust and spiderwebs, with a large open book. Doña Judith approached it and read the pages, discovering that it was a black magic grimoire. Before she could continue reading, the shadow reappeared and revealed itself to be the Marquise of Linares.

The Marquise confessed that she was a descendant of the woman in the portrait, a powerful sorceress who had been condemned to wander the castle as a vengeful spirit. She explained to Doña Judith that she came to fetch her ancestor's grimoire.

In another corner of the castle, the Count of Valdemar discovered that his taunts and challenges were in vain. Terrified, he found himself face to face with an impressive spectre, dressed in deep red, chasing him through the hallway. The souls of the castle were starting to awaken.

While the Marquise of Linares was telling Doña Judith the real reason for their meeting in the castle, the other guests also began to encounter the spirits that inhabited the place.

Throughout the corridors and rooms, the fearsome spectres manifested themselves, casting ancient curses and revealing their secrets.

The Count of Valdemar, seized by terror, managed to escape from the spectre that was chasing him and ran to warn the others.

In his flight, he ran into Doña Judith and the Marquise, who told him what they had discovered in the hidden chamber. Together, they decided they must face Don Rodrigo and demand an explanation.

Armed with their knowledge of the truth and fear of what might happen to them if they did not act, the group set out to confront Don Rodrigo.

They found him in the library, reading another ancient book of spells. When confronted, he admitted that the curse was real and that he brought his guests to the castle to offer their souls to the spirits.

The guests, terrified by the apparitions, tried to find a way to escape from the castle, but all the doors and windows were locked by dark magic. The atmosphere in the castle was becoming more and more oppressive and sinister, and the spirits were being increasingly aggressive and violent.

The Count of Valdemar picked up one of the medieval swords that decorated the walls and lunged at Don Rodrigo. He thrust the sword into his chest and Don Rodrigo fell dead.

Doña Judith and the Marquise watched the scene in horror. The Count, whose eyes were red, drew the sword from Don Rodrigo and rushed at them, murdering them with it.

The rest of the guests were also fighting, killing each other, throwing each other down the stairs, stabbing each other with dinner knives, in an orgy of blood. No one survived.

The next morning, Friar Juan returned to the castle. The door could now be opened. The friar looked horrified at what had happened, all was full of blood and corpses.

The wailing passage

The night of *Samhain* had fallen over Dublin, and darkness loomed over the Earth. Einar, Freydis, Bjorn and their Viking comrades were in the city, eager to explore and understand the customs and legends of the mysterious Ireland. Freydis was curious about the people who walked the streets, telling stories of spirits and supernatural beings.

At a local inn, the Vikings encountered Sinead and Aedan, two Irish brothers who seemed intrigued by the newcomers.

As they struck up conversation, Sinead shared the legend of the Wailing Passage, an ancient tunnel hidden beneath the city that was said to be inhabited by a dark spirit that fed on the fear and despair of those who dared to enter its abode.

Aedan, the druid, confirmed the story emphatically. He spoke of how, during *Samhain*, the veil between the world of the living and the dead became thinner, allowing evil spirits to cross over into the earthly world. The wailing passage, he said, was a place of great power and danger, especially on that night.

Einar, defiant, could not help but be attracted by the story and proposed to explore the passage, convinced that his courage and skill would protect him from danger. Freydis, though concerned, decided to join him, confident in her skills as a seer and healer. Bjorn, fearful but loyal, could not leave his friends alone on such a risky adventure.

Sinead and Aedan reluctantly agreed to lead the Vikings to the entrance of the passage, but they warned them that they could not guarantee their safety once inside. Together, the group set off into the darkness of the night, committed to confront the mystery of the wailing passage and, perhaps, discover the truth behind the legend.

In the moonlight, they led the group through the narrow streets of Dublin, away from the bustle of the city centre to a wooded hill on the outskirts. The trees rustled in the wind, and the air was filled with a thick, oppressive energy that weighed heavily on their shoulders.

They followed the brothers to an entrance hidden among the roots of an ancient oak tree, barely visible to the naked eye. Aedan spoke a few words in Gaelic, and the entrance was revealed, exposing a dark passage leading into the depths of the earth.

Upon reaching the threshold of the passageway, Sinead extracted a handful of protective herbs and handed them to the Vikings. He explained that they should carry them throughout the journey, for they might be their only defence against the evil forces lurking inside the tunnel. Einar, Freydis and Bjorn accepted the herbs gratefully, and the brothers wished them luck before withdrawing, leaving them alone in the darkness.

Carrying torches and their weapons, the Vikings began to descend the passage, feeling the air grow colder and wetter as they went. The stone walls were covered with mould, and the ground was uneven and slippery, making it difficult to advance.

Freydis, with her seer powers, sensed the presence of something dark and malevolent watching them from the shadows. She tried to communicate with the spirit, but her attempts were in vain. The entity fed on the fear and uncertainty growing in the hearts of the group.

As they went deeper into the passageway, the wailing of the tormented spirits filled the air, echoing off the walls and ringing in their ears. Though they could not see the souls in pain, they could feel their suffering, and a shiver ran through their bodies.

With each step the wailing of the spirits became louder, and the atmosphere grew even more distressing. Freydis began to mutter words of protection under her breath, trying to keep the dark forces around them at bay.

Suddenly, the torches went out, leaving the Vikings in total darkness. Freydis hastily lit a new torch, revealing a hidden chamber at the heart of the passage. The walls of the chamber were covered with ancient Celtic symbols and Norse runes, and in the centre was a stone altar on which rested an amulet emitting a powerful energy.

The three approached the altar, and Freydis felt a vile presence stronger than ever. It was then that the evil spirit appeared, a tall, dark, long-armed, hooded figure with burning eyes and an evil expression. At its feet lay the tormented souls that had been imprisoned there.

The creature noticed that they were carrying protective herbs, so instead of attacking them, it challenged them to a game of wits, promising to free the souls and allow them to leave if they could solve its riddles. However, if they failed, their souls would be trapped in the passageway forever, as happened to the others.

Bravely, the Vikings accepted the challenge, the evil spirit would present each of them with a riddle to solve. The first riddle was:

'Smoke on the fireless mountain.'

Einar, Freydis and Bjorn took some time to reflect, realising that the riddle was connected to the amulet and the symbols that covered the walls of the chamber.

Freydis, using her skills as a seer, concentrated on the runes and the amulet, searching for the answer to the riddle. With each failed attempt, the evil spirit's smile grew, and time was rapidly running out. But then, in a moment of clarity, Freydis found the solution to the riddle and shouted the answer at the top of her lungs:

'Fog!'

The evil spirit writhed in rage. After a few moments he smiled again and spoke the second riddle:

'A bridge over the lake, it has neither wood nor stone.'

The Vikings thought about what it could be. All the bridges they knew had wood in them. After a few moments, Einar exclaimed:

'Ice!'

The spirit had underestimated the Vikings, but he was still confident that they would not guess the third riddle:

'It's neither outside nor inside, yet it's very important in the house.'

It was Bjorn's turn, but his mind was blank, he couldn't think of anything. The spirit already saw itself victorious. Freydis and Einar reached for their weapons as the creature grew in size. Suddenly, Bjorn shouted:

'Door!'

After pronouncing the third answer, the amulet on the altar started to glow brightly. Freydis grasped it in her hands and read a Gaelic phrase that appeared on the object. The evil spirit was consumed by the power of the amulet and disappeared in a whirlwind of darkness.

With the wicked spirit defeated, they felt a change in the atmosphere of the passageway. The oppression that once filled the air vanished, and the wailing of the spirits slowly began to subside. Freydis, still holding the glowing amulet in her hands, turned to the trapped souls and spoke words of deliverance in the ancient tongue of the druids.

The souls, once trapped in eternal torment, began to rise from the ground and fade away in a soft light. As the souls were being freed, the Vikings could feel a sense of peace and gratitude emanating from them. The three watched in humility as the souls left the passageway and made their way to their final resting place.

Still, they knew they could not stay there forever. With the amulet in their power, they began to search for a way out of the passage. As they advanced, they noticed that the Celtic symbols and Norse runes on the walls began to fade, erased by the liberating power of the amulet.

Eventually, the Vikings found a ladder that led them to the surface. They emerged in a clearing in the forest, under the moonlight. The three returned to their camp, relieved that their adventure in Irish lands was over. No doubt they preferred the plundering to which they were accustomed.

The screams of the possessed doll

The *okiya* in Kyoto was known for its elegance and the beauty of its residents. Aiko, a talented young geisha, strived to be the best in her art, attracting the attention of many admirers, including Haruki, a young samurai who visited her frequently.

On the first day of Obon, a mysterious package arrived at the geisha house, addressed to Aiko. Inside the box, she found an exquisitely detailed porcelain doll, dressed in a beautiful kimono. No one knew who had sent the doll, but Aiko was fascinated by its beauty and placed it in her room as a decoration.

The *okiya* was filled with whispers and rumours about the doll. Hana, an experienced geisha and Aiko's close friend of, told her about an old local legend that spoke of dolls possessed by vengeful spirits.

Aiko, though intrigued, did not pay much attention to the story. That same night, however, the geisha house was disrupted by the sound of bloodcurdling screams that seemed to come from Aiko's room.

Sayuri, the *okāsan* or matriarch of the house, ran to investigate along with the apprentices *maiko* and geisha. On arriving at Aiko's room, they found the young girl paralysed with fear, pointing to the doll on the shelf. The doll, which once wore a serene expression, now had a sinister smile on its face.

The next morning, Sayuri took the doll to an old woman knowledgeable in the spiritual and supernatural. After a careful examination, the *obāsan* revealed that the doll was possessed by a *yūrei*, a vengeful spirit, a woman who had suffered a tragedy in her past life.

Meanwhile, Aiko, still dismayed by the events of the previous night, was visited by Haruki, who heard what happened. Concerned for her safety, Haruki promised to protect her from danger.

The *okiya was* filled with an atmosphere of tension and fear. The women began to experience strange occurrences, such as objects moving on their own and noises in the shadows. Sayuri, committed to protect her geisha and lift the curse, consulted the *obāsan* again.

The old woman explained that the spirit of the *yūrei* would only find peace if a proper funeral ceremony was performed for it. However, she also warned that it had to be done properly, or the curse would get worse.

Sayuri and the geisha prepared themselves to perform the ceremony that same evening, with Haruki offering his help. Everyone feared what might happen if something went wrong, but they were willing to face their fears in order to free themselves from the *yūrei*.

On the night of the funeral, everyone gathered in the inner courtyard of the house. Under the dim light of paper lamps, they prepared an altar with offerings for the spirit. The atmosphere was heavy and tense, and everyone feared what might happen if it went wrong.

The *obāsan* led the ceremony, reciting an ancient *sutra* while all present concentrated on appeasing the vengeful spirit. The doll, placed in the centre of the altar, seemed more sinister than ever, and its presence made everyone uneasy.

As the ceremony progressed, the strange phenomena intensified. Objects flew around the room, and the screams of the possessed doll echoed in the air. Haruki, though worried for Aiko and the other geisha, stood firm and brave.

At the climax of the ceremony, the *obāsan* spoke the final words and everyone held their breath, waiting for the curse to dissipate. But something went terribly wrong. Instead of vanishing, the doll's evil energy grew, and the spirit of the *yūrei* appeared in front of them, furious and more powerful than ever.

The *yūrei*, now materialised and more menacing than ever, was a terrifying and macabre figure. Its appearance sent shivers down the spine of even the bravest of hearts. It was a spectral entity with disfigured features and an appearance that denoted its extreme suffering. Her face was white, full of cuts. Her hair was long and tangled, from which her evil thoughts sprouted. Her eyes were two empty sockets. She wore an ancient kimono that waved in the air, as if she were trapped in a vortex of eternal suffering. As he moved, his limbs twisted unnaturally. Her long, bony, disfigured fingers ended in sharp, ghostly claws.

While approaching, it emitted a piercing, guttural wail that shook the souls of those unfortunate enough to find themselves in its presence. It embodied the accumulated horror and evil of years of abuse, and its very existence was a manifestation of the deepest terrors of the human psyche.

It began to wreak havoc in the *okiya*. Walls shook and doors slammed violently as the spirit's scream filled the air. In desperation, the geisha, Haruki and the *obāsan* sought refuge in different parts of the house, hoping to find a solution to appease the *yūrei*'s fury.

Sayuri and the *obāsan* tried to contain the chaos that had been unleashed in the house. Using their knowledge of the spiritual and supernatural, they tried to protect the geisha and weaken the strength of the *yūrei*, but with little success.

Aiko, terrified and struggling to remain calm, recalled the *obāsan*'s words about the tragedy in the *yūrei*'s past life. She told Haruki that the *yūrei* had been a young geisha who was betrayed by her companions and mistreated since she was a *maiko*. The girl committed suicide and her spirit was trapped in the doll, where her rage had grown over the years. Together with Haruki, they decided that exposing the truth behind her suffering might be the key to stopping her.

Time was running against them and the geisha house was on the brink of destruction, Aiko and Haruki devised a plan to free the spirit and put an end to its wrath once and for all. Aiko, her heart full of compassion, spoke aloud to the *yūrei*:

'I know the truth about your past and the betrayal you have suffered!'

As Aiko told the story, the *yūrei's* fury began to subside slowly, leaving room to the sadness and despair she had felt for years. But the dark energy surrounding the *yūrei* fought fiercely to keep her trapped in her prison of hatred and vengeance. Then, Haruki intervened:

'Don't let hatred rule you. We respect your art and what you were. Don't give power to those who envied you!'

Finally, with a burst of light, the link was broken and the spirit was released. With a final sigh, it disappeared, leaving behind the inert doll and a sense of peace in the *okiya*. It was all over.

The group breathed a sigh of relief and could now return to their lives. Aiko picked up the doll. It still had that sinister smile on its face.

The ghosts of the hospital

Night was falling over Huelva in the year 2000, and a group of six teenagers gathered at Álvaro's house, eager to begin their adventure in the abandoned Manuel Lois hospital. All Hallows' Eve was in full swing, and the youngsters could not think of a more terrifying place to spend it.

Marta, who had previously investigated the hospital, shared with the group horror stories and paranormal events that occurred there, increasing their nervousness.

Still, fear did not stop them from preparing for the exciting adventure. They loaded their backpacks with torches, extra batteries, a camera and supplies, willing to face the unknown.

Once ready, the six friends began to walk towards the abandoned hospital. As they approached, the dark silhouette of the huge building loomed before them, casting an eerie shadow over the group. The full moon lit the way, but clouds threatened to obscure it at any moment.

When they reached the outskirts of the hospital, Matias couldn't help but shudder at the sight of the huge structure. The broken windows and damp walls made it look even creepier. Álvaro, always brave, took the initiative and opened the rusty iron gate leading to the hospital.

Once inside, the darkness was almost total. They turned on their torches and began to explore the long, narrow corridors, filled with debris and remnants of a forgotten past. Rocío, feeling the energy of the place, shuddered as she sensed a supernatural presence.

Sergio, trying to ease the tension, began to tell jokes and make fun of the ghosts, but his humour only increased Matias' fear, who kept looking back, afraid that something might follow them.

As they walked down the corridor, Carmen took notes in her journal, jotting down every detail and observation she made. However, Carmen's curiosity was not shared by everyone, and some of her friends were more concerned about what they might find in the hospital than solving its mysteries.

Thus, the group of teenagers slowly made their way through the abandoned hospital, unaware that they would soon be confronted with the horrors they had heard in stories and the ghosts that, according to legend, roamed the dark hallways of the building.

The friends continued moving deeper into the abandoned hospital, exploring the rooms and common areas that were once bustling with hustle. In one of the rooms, they found an old wheelchair, covered in dust and cobwebs. Rocío, who felt more and more the presence of the supernatural, approached the chair and gingerly touched it, feeling her blood run cold.

At that moment, a shuddering scream broke the silence. Startled they ran to where the scream had come from. There they found Matias, trembling and with eyes full of terror, pointing down a corridor. As they looked, they all saw the figure of a young woman, pale-faced, with long black hair, dressed in a white nightgown, illuminated by a mysterious light that seemed to come from nowhere. As they pointed their torches at her, she disappeared.

The group gasped, unable to believe what they just witnessed. Sergio, trying to regain his composure, attempted to convince the others that it was just an illusion, what they call a collective hallucination, caused by the suggestion of the place. But he failed to dispel their fear.

They moved on, but with a renewed sense of caution and apprehension. They explored the old operating theatre, where they found rusty surgical instruments and dark stains on the floor that seemed blood. They began to hear whispers all around them, as if the hospital walls were speaking to them.

The murmurs grew louder and louder and seemed to come from all directions. Álvaro, who was brave until now, began to feel panic take hold of him. He could not understand what the whispers were saying, but he sensed that they were trying to warn them or drive them away from the place.

Carmen, trying to stay calm, suggested to start communicating with the spirits using the Ouija board she had brought in her backpack. They sat in a circle on the floor of one of the rooms and placed the Ouija board in the centre. With trembling hands, they placed their fingers on the glass and began to ask questions.

They waited anxiously and fearfully for the glass to start moving on the board. The first question they asked was whether there was anyone there with them, and to their horror, the glass moved quickly towards "YES".

The sounds around them seemed to increase in intensity, and each of the friends felt a tightness in their chests, as if something was making it difficult to breathe. Ignoring their growing fear, they continued to ask questions with the esoteric board. They asked who was he and what did he want from them, but the glass moved from letter to letter without forming coherent words.

Then, Rocío impulsively asked the spirits if they were in danger. The glass slowly slid towards "YES", that very moment, a gust of icy wind blew across the room, turning off their torches and leaving them in complete darkness.

The group screamed and tried to turn their torches back on, but the batteries seemed to have run out. The whispers turned to ominous laughter and piercing wails, and the friends felt terror envelop them like a cold, heavy blanket.

Then, a clear, penetrating voice emerged through the noises, uttering the words:

'You must go... Now!'

The friends didn't need to hear any more. They got up and started running towards the exit, stumbling in the darkness and calling out to each other not to get lost. The doors slammed shut behind them, and the shadows seemed to come alive, trying to catch them. Wailing and laughter followed, making them feel as if they were being hunted by unseen, malevolent forces.

Finally, they reached the main entrance of the hospital, but the door was locked and did not seem to yield to their efforts to open it.

Exhausted and on the verge of collapse, they realised that they would have to find another way out or face the wrath of the spirits that inhabited the Manuel Lois Hospital.

With the front door closed, the friends decided to split into two groups to increase their chances of finding a way out. Rocío, Álvaro and Sergio headed towards the west wing of the hospital, while Matias, Carmen and Marta explored the east wing.

The west wing was in worse condition than the rest of the hospital. The rooms and corridors were littered with debris and the remains of medical equipment. As they moved on, Rocío, Álvaro and Sergio felt as if something was watching them from the shadows, and the wailing and laughter continued to haunt them.

Suddenly, they found a door ajar leading to a backyard. Without hesitation, they burst the door open and stepped outside. But their relief was short-lived, as they realised they were trapped in a maze of high walls and narrow corridors.

Meanwhile, Matias, Carmen and Marta had no better luck in the east wing. They also felt the presence of evil spirits haunting them. In one room, they found an old map of the hospital with an emergency exit marked in the radiology area.

With renewed hope they set off, but as they drew nearer, the hissing and wailing intensified, and a sense of dread came over them. Despite their fears, they pressed on, thinking it was their only hope of escape.

Rocío, Álvaro and Sergio finally found a way out of the maze that led them right in front of the radiology area. They heard the voices of their friends and followed them.

All together again, they discovered an old metal door, very big and heavy. Without a second thought, they opened the door, praying that it would lead them away from the terror of the hospital.

The door led into a hallway that was dark and damp. They walked together in silence, fearing that the spirits of the hospital might follow them even there.

Halfway through, they found another door, this one made of wood. Behind it, there was a small room full of personal belongings, photographs and documents, as if someone had been living there.

Among the documents, they discovered the truth behind the hospital ghosts: the spirit that had been haunting them was actually a former hospital employee, an orderly named Antonio, who had died in a tragic accident. After his death, his soul had found no rest and had been terrorising intruders who dared to enter the abandoned hospital.

Finally, the teenagers reached the end of the long corridor and found their way outside. They escaped from the hospital just as the sun began to rise over the horizon. Exhausted but happy, they promised themselves never to enter abandoned and haunted places again, especially on *Tosantos*.

As they drove away from the hospital, a gentle breeze blew through the broken windows and open doors, carrying with it the wailing of the trapped spirit.

The hotel of terror

Emily Thompson, a young journalist, arrived at the Hotel Cilce on a rainy October afternoon. Drawn by the stories of murders, disappearances and mysterious deaths surrounding the hotel, Emily decided to investigate the strange goings-on for herself.

With her friend Laura Mitchell and Detective Richards, she hoped to unravel the hotel's murky secrets and write a story that would launch her to journalistic stardom.

As soon as Emily crossed the doors of the hotel, she felt a little dizzy. The lobby was decorated with antiques and tapestries that seemed to be from another era. The air was heavy with a musty smell and an atmosphere that was hard to describe. The three made their way to the front desk to check in, where they met the enigmatic Mr. Johnson, the hotel manager.

Mr. Johnson welcomed them with a forced smile and handed them their room keys. While Emily was signing the register, she noticed the manager watching her carefully, as if he knew why she came to the hotel.

When asked about paranormal occurrences, Mr. Johnson was evasive and advised them to enjoy their stay at the hotel without worrying about "unsubstantiated rumours".

With some discomfort, the three of them went up to their respective rooms and began to settle in. As they unpacked, Emily couldn't help but feel something strange about the place, a kind of attraction. The walls seemed to hold secrets, and the air was filled with an eerie energy.

In the evening, the trio met in the hotel bar to discuss their research plan. While they were drinking and sharing their concerns, a man who overheard them, named Peter Harris, approached.

Peter told them that he was also staying at the Cilce Hotel and had experienced strange phenomena. He decided to join the group in their search for answers.

After a long conversation, Emily and Laura returned to their room, while Richards and Peter retired to theirs.

But sleep didn't come easily. In the middle of the night, Emily heard footsteps in the hallway and mumbling in her room.

She was sure she was not alone and that something strange and frightening lurked in the shadows of the hotel.

The next morning, everyone met in the hotel dining room for breakfast. They shared their experiences of the previous night, and though some had not noticed anything strange, Emily couldn't forget the feeling that someone or something had been watching her while asleep.

After breakfast, the group decided to split up to investigate the common areas of the hotel and interview other guests.

Emily and Laura headed to the library, while Richards and Peter explored the basement and corridors of the hotel.

In the library, the two girls met a woman named Marjorie, who told them about her experience. She had seen a shadowy figure in her room the night before and was visibly frightened. She confessed that she didn't dare to spend another night in the hotel.

Emily took note of her account and they continued their investigation.

Meanwhile, Richards and Peter discovered a series of locked rooms in the basement. By forcing the door of one of them, they found a room full of personal belongings of guests who had disappeared in the hotel.

Among the items, they found diaries describing encounters with supernatural entities and descriptions of terrifying dreams.

That night, Emily and Laura decided to stay awake in their room to try and capture some paranormal phenomenon.

As the night wore on, they began to hear creaking and banging sounds in the walls. Although scared, they wanted evidence, so they recorded the sounds with their devices.

Suddenly, a cold wind started to blow in the room and a dark figure appeared at the side of the bed.

Paralysed with fear, the women could barely breathe as the figure slowly approached them.

Before it could touch them, the figure vanished into thin air, leaving them terrified but unharmed.

In the morning, they both told what happened to Richards and Peter, who spent the night searching the locked basement rooms.

The four decided to investigate the city's historical archives and interview the hotel employees in search of clues. They discovered that the hotel had a long history of tragic deaths, murders and suicides dating back to its opening in the 1920s.

Among the most notorious cases, they discovered the murder of a young woman named Emma, whose mutilated body was found on the roof of the hotel. Emma was a beautiful and mysterious woman who had stayed at the hotel before her disappearance, and many believed that her spirit still roamed the corridors of the Cilce.

They also discovered that during the 1930s and 1940s, the hotel was a meeting place for underworld figures and members of the mafia. Violence and corruption left a deep mark on the Cilce, and its employees shared stories of unsolved crimes and mysterious disappearances.

While investigating the hotel's past, Emily and Laura interviewed a former concierge named Walter, who told them about a series of secret tunnels that connected the hotel to other nearby buildings.

These tunnels, according to Walter, had been used by members of the mafia to escape the police and carry out their illegal activities in secret. He also confessed that there were rumours of satanic rituals and occult practices taking place in the hotel.

With this new information, the group decided to explore the tunnels in search for answers. With torches and cameras, they descended to the last floor and began to wander the dark underground passages. The sounds of wailing and whispers seemed to follow them, increasing their fear.

At the end of one of the tunnels, they found a hidden room that appeared to have been used for occult rituals. There were strange symbols painted on the walls and floor, triangles and grotesque figures, as well as mysterious objects and ash on the bed.

As they examined the room, Emily felt a shiver and suddenly, the spectre of Emma appeared before them, with an expression of pain and suffering on her face.

Before they could react, the figure disappeared, leaving the group with more questions than answers.

Convinced that the hotel was plagued by vengeful spirits and dark forces, they turned to a paranormal expert, Dr. Abraham Wallace.

Dr. Wallace, a scholar of the occult, had spent years investigating paranormal phenomena and helping free people and places of negative energies. When the group told him what they had experienced at the hotel, he agreed to investigate the case and help them in their quest to unravel the mystery of the Cilce.

Geared up with specialised equipment to detect and combat paranormal forces, they returned to the hotel. They decided to split into groups to cover more ground. Dr. Wallace and Peter would explore the basement and tunnels, while Emily, Laura and Richards would investigate the hotel rooms and corridors.

At every step of their search, the paranormal phenomena intensified. In the basement, Dr. Wallace and Peter found a number of objects that seemed to have been used in dark rituals. Meanwhile, in the bedrooms, the others witnessed apparitions and heard screams and moans that seemed to come from the walls.

After hours of research, the two groups met in the hotel lobby to share their findings. Emily, however, did not show up. No one knew where she was. Suddenly, they heard a ruckus in the street and the sounds of sirens. They stepped outside and discovered the lifeless body of Emily, who apparently had thrown herself from the hotel roof.

The group was in shock. Dr. Wallace was convinced that the hotel was under a powerful curse and they would need to perform a cleansing ritual to rid it of the sinister forces occupying it.

They prepared the ritual according to Dr. Wallace's instructions. In the centre of the lobby, they formed a pentacle with salt and lit candles. Dr. Wallace began reciting the texts from an ancient book, asking the spirits to leave the hotel and return to the afterlife.

As he chanted, the hotel began to shake and the lights flickered. But it was no earthquake. The spirits, including the figure of Emma, appeared before them, visibly angry and reluctant to leave the place. Furniture shook, lamps swayed wildly, and mirrors creaked as if they were about to shatter. The air was filled with an icy cold. Doors slammed open and shut on their own, curtains fluttered as if whipped by an invisible wind, and whispering voices filled the room with moans and groans.

Stoically, Dr. Wallace continued the ritual. Little by little, the spirits began to fade away and, after a long struggle, the atmosphere in the Cilce Hotel changed. The heavy and anxious air was gone, the employees and guests began to feel a sense of peace and relief.

Yet, the team could not forget the loss of Emily. They never really knew what happened to her. Security cameras recorded her climbing up to the roof, seemingly running away from something or someone. According to hotel staff, the young reporter is still wandering the hallway of the Cilce.

The curse of the empty house

Xavier Carbonell looked across the street at the empty house. The imposing structure, whose brick walls seemed to hold many secrets, stood on a hill on the outskirts of Madrid. He heard rumours of a curse hanging over the property, and though he was sceptical, his curiosity as a writer of mystery and horror novels prompted him to investigate.

That afternoon, his daughter Montserrat accompanied him in his search for inspiration. Despite her youth, the teenager shared her father's interest in the unknown and the supernatural.

Together they walked into the neglected garden surrounding the house. As they approached, an uneasy feeling began to take hold of them.

Xavier knocked on the front door, and to his surprise, it opened slowly with a chilling screech. Cautiously, father and daughter entered the house, their footsteps echoing in the sepulchral silence. Once inside, they found themselves in a wide hallway that led to several rooms covered in dust and spiderwebs.

As they explored the house, they couldn't help but feel like something was watching them from the shadows. The rooms seemed to be trapped in time, with old furniture and personal items bearing witness to the lives that once inhabited the place. Father and daughter grew increasingly restless as they walked through the house, but their curiosity drove them on.

It was then that they met Lucía Jiménez, a local journalist who had been investigating the empty house for months. Lucía told them the tragic story of Mariana, the woman whose spirit was supposedly linked to the house's curse. Together, they decided to join forces to uncover the truth behind the mysterious property.

That night, while Xavier and Montserrat returned home, they couldn't help but feel that something had changed. The encounter with the empty house and Mariana's story had affected them deeply. What once seemed to be only a search for inspiration for Xavier had now become an obsession that threatened to consume them.

And as the full moon illuminated the house on the hill, the shadows seemed to move and whisper, as if waiting for the right moment to reveal their dark secrets.

Xavier spent the next few days investigating the history of the empty house. With the help of his daughter and Lucía, he began to discover dark and forgotten secrets dating back decades. Meanwhile, the haunting presence of the house seemed to extend beyond its walls, affecting those who had dared to explore it.

One day, while going through records in the library, Xavier met Santiago, an old childhood friend who was now working as a history teacher in Madrid. Santiago had also heard about the empty house and was intrigued by the curse that seemed to surround it. Together, they began to investigate the history of the property, trying to unravel the mystery.

At the same time, Montserrat had befriended Andrés, an elderly neighbour of the empty house who had lived in the area all his life. He shared stories of his youth, when he and his friends dared to explore the house and experienced strange and inexplicable occurrences. Although kind and helpful, Montserrat could not help but feel that the old man was hiding something about his past and his connection to the house.

As the group delved deeper into the history of the house and its former inhabitants, they began to find clues about a curse that had been unleashed decades before. Strange and tragic events seemed to follow those who dared to live in the house, and the shadow of Mariana, the woman whose spirit was linked to the curse, loomed over each of them.

One night, while Xavier and Lucía were going through old documents in the library, they came across a manuscript that belonged to Mariana. The yellowed and worn-out pages revealed her innermost thoughts and fears, as well as her encounters with dark forces that seemed to stalk her from the shadows. As they read, a feeling of horror and sympathy began to take hold of them. One particularly shocking paragraph read:

'The shadows that haunt this house are not mere illusions or ghosts. I feel their presence, their cold breath on my nape when darkness falls. I pray every night for protection, but I fear my soul has already been marked by the unknown. Who are these beings that whisper in the night and mock my sanity? I pray for light, but I fear that the curse of this house is more powerful than I can ever comprehend.'

To unravel the mystery of the empty house and put an end to the curse, Xavier suggested seeking the help of a medium named Luis. His ability to communicate with the afterlife and his knowledge of magic could be the key to uncovering the truth behind the curse and freeing Mariana and the house from the shadows that tormented them.

Thus, on a stormy night, the five gathered in the empty house, preparing to face the darkness that awaited them. But what they didn't know was that their actions would trigger a series of events that would endanger themselves and everyone they knew.

They stepped into the house, each with what courage he could muster to face the mystery that lurked within. The air was charged with electricity, as if the atmosphere itself knew that something important was about to happen.

Luis began preparing for the spiritual session, placing candles in a circle around a table in the centre of the living room. The group sat, holding hands, as Luis invoked the spirits that inhabited the house. Silence fell over the place, broken only by the creaking of wood and the rustle of the wind outside.

Suddenly, a cold, invisible presence filled the room. Candles flickered and shadows seemed to move like serpents along the walls. Luis, his voice trembling but firm, addressed the spirits, asking them about the curse and how they could free Mariana.

The answer came in the form of a barely audible spectral voice, which seemed to come from all directions at once. Mariana, the tragic woman linked to the house, revealed that she had been the victim of a black magic session, carried out by a group of people seeking power. The ceremony had unleashed an evil force in the house, trapping Mariana's spirit and plunging the property into a curse that would last for eternity.

Listening to Mariana's spirit tell her tragic tale, the group felt even more determined to put an end to the curse and free her from its torment. But how could they do this? What would they have to face to break the spell that enveloped the empty house?

Mariana disclosed that in order to free her and break the curse, they had to find and destroy a cursed object that had been hidden somewhere in the house during the session.

This object, a harmless-looking wooden carving, contained the very essence of the evil force that tormented the house and her spirit.

With hearts pounding and commitment in their eyes, the group began their search through the house, turning every corner and poking into every crevice in search of the carving. What they didn't know was that the dark force inhabiting the house had no intention of letting them find it, and that the struggle to free Mariana and break the curse of the empty house would test their courage and will to survive.

The night was far from over, and the shadows in the empty house seemed to move and writhe. The search for the cursed carving became increasingly intense as everyone went through the house. Every room and corridor seemed to hide a secret, and the sense of darkness stalking them grew stronger with every step they took.

After hours of fruitless searching, Lucía, tired and frustrated, stumbled upon a room hidden behind a bookshelf in the library.

The chamber, covered in dust and cobwebs, was crammed with ancient objects and relics of a shadowy past. And there, in a small brass box in the centre of the room, they found the cursed carving.

The object had a sinister appearance, with a symbol engraved on its surface that seemed to change and move as they looked at it. The evil it emanated was palpable, and everyone in the group felt a shiver run down their spine as they touched it.

Luis, the medium, explained that in order to destroy the carving and break the curse, they had to carry out another magic session in the same place where the dark rite that created it had been performed.

Guided by Mariana's spirit, the group went to the attic of the house. It was an eerie room, surrounded by skulls. There was also an altar, a book and candles. Lightning was streaming in through a small window in the ceiling.

As the wind howled and the rain pelted the windows, they began the session to destroy the carving. They lit all the candles in the room and, as they recited the words of the book in a forgotten language, the atmosphere of the house shifted. The darkness that had been stalking them seemed to concentrate in one point, ready to defend its existence at all costs.

An unseen force rushed over the group, slamming and throwing them against the walls in an attempt to stop the session. One of the candles fell on the tablecloth, which started to burn. With a final cry of defiance, Luis threw the wooden carving into the fire.

A howl full of fury and despair echoed through the house as the carving was consumed by flames. The darkness lifted, and the sense of oppression and terror that had followed the group since their arrival at the house vanished.

As the sun set and the group prepared to leave, a gentle breeze blew through the empty house, carrying with it the scent of fresh flowers and a sense of tranquillity. In that moment, everyone knew that Mariana's spirit was grateful and finally at peace.

Exhausted and relieved, they departed the empty house, leaving behind the curse and the darkness that had tormented Mariana and all those who dared to enter the property.

They spent the rest of the day together, sharing their experiences and reflecting on the supernatural events that had united them in an unbreakable friendship. Luis, the medium, grateful for their courage and perseverance, assured them he would always be at their disposal if they ever needed his help again.

Life in Madrid returned to normal, but the shared experience in the house left an indelible mark on each of them. Xavier, Lucía, Montserrat and Santiago remained close friends, supporting one another in the challenges that life presented them with. Andrés, the elderly neighbour, also found solace in the resolution of the mystery and was able to live the rest of his days without the burden of the past that tormented him.

The empty house was restored and, in time, became a warm and welcoming home for a new family who never knew the terror that had once inhabited it. Yet, the stories of the house's curse would continue to be told for years to come.

The garden of living statues

In ancient Rome, the city was a hive of activity and wealth. Its streets were filled with busy citizens and merchants from all over the world. In the midst of all this bustle, Lucius Verus, a brave young centurion, walked steadily through the cobbled streets towards the home of his friend Flavia Augusta.

Flavia had invited Lucius to her luxurious villa, where they were holding the Pomona festival. When he arrived, he was greeted by a crowd of guests, all dressed in their best robes and finery. As he walked through the hall, Lucius could not help but admire the impressive marble statues that adorned the place.

At one point, Flavia approached Lucius and suggested a stroll through the garden to escape the noise of the party.

As they walked among the neatly trimmed hedges and colourful flowers, Lucius couldn't help but notice a strange feeling overcome him.

'Flavia, who is the sculptor of these magnificent statues?' he asked, impressed by the realism of the works.

'It's Tiberius, a very talented elderly man. But there is something peculiar about his work,' Flavia confessed, lowering her voice. 'There are rumours that his statues come alive in the dark of night.'

Lucius frowned, intrigued but sceptical at the idea.

'These are only rumours, Flavia. You needn't worry about them,' Lucius said, trying to allay her fears.

At that moment, the sun began to set, and shadows fell across the garden. Lucius and Flavia decided to return to the party, but as they turned around, they noticed something strange: a statue seemed to have changed position since they last saw it.

Uneasy, the two friends hurried to get back inside, but something stopped them. An almost inaudible whisper seemed to emanate from a nearby statue. Lucius approached cautiously, and the whisper became a piercing wail that froze the blood in his veins.

They looked at each other, and a shared fear shined in their eyes. In that moment, they knew that the rumours of the living statues were not mere tales, but something far more terrifying and mysterious. Eager to know more, Lucius and Flavia went into the garden.

With their hearts racing, they moved slowly among the statues, listening for every little movement and sound. The moon, now high in the night sky, bathed the garden in silver light, creating shapes that seemed to take on a life of their own.

Suddenly, a hooded figure emerged from the shadows, holding a torch that illuminated his wrinkled and tired face. It was Tiberius, the old sculptor.

'What are you young people doing here? Don't you know that this garden is not safe at night?' he warned them sternly.

'Tiberius, we heard the wailing of the statues,' said Flavia, her voice trembling. Please tell us what's happening.

The old man sighed deeply and, after a moment's silence, began to tell his story.

'Years ago, on a journey to the distant lands of Egypt, I found an ancient scroll that contained a magic spell. It said that if I spoke it while carving a statue, it would come to life and grant me supernatural abilities. Desperate to achieve perfection in my art, I recited the spell and, since then, all my creations have been possessed by the souls of people.'

Flavia and Lucius, struck by the revelation, exchanged worried glances.

'And how can we break the spell?' asked Lucius.

'I don't know,' Tiberius replied ruefully. 'I have searched for years, but the scroll was lost, and I have found no solution.'

Right then, a nearby statue began to move slowly. Its features twisted into a pained expression, and its eyes, now alive, pleaded for help.

The terrifying scene convinced Lucius and Flavia to free the trapped souls. They joined forces with Tiberius to find a way to end the spell that tormented the statues.

The three began their search at the villa of Senator Marcus Caelius, a cultured man and lover of the arts. They knew that his extensive collection of books and scrolls was their best chance of finding some clue on how to break the enchantment.

As they perused the scrolls and shelves, Flavia found an ancient book that told the story of a spell similar to the one Tiberius had described. The book spoke of a potion that could reverse the effects and free the trapped souls.

The potion required several elements: a tear of the moon, the heart of a lion and the dust of a shooting star. These ingredients were to be mixed and sprinkled on the statues during the full moon.

Even if the task seemed almost impossible, the trio was not willing to give up. They split up to gather the necessary elements before the next full moon. Lucius would search for a lion's heart, while Flavia would go looking for the dust of a shooting star.

Tiberius, who knew of a lake outside Rome where the tears of the moon were said to fall, arranged for the last ingredient. Each of them set off for their destination, knowing that if they failed to gather the elements, the souls trapped in the statues would be condemned to eternal suffering.

As the full moon approached, the tension increased and the statues in the garden became increasingly restless. Lucius, Flavia and Tiberius managed to gather the necessary ingredients for the potion. They met in the garden of the living statues under the moonlight.

With the heart of a lion, the dust of a shooting star and the tear of the moon in their hands, they prepared the magic mixture according to the instructions in the ancient book. As they mixed the ingredients, an unearthly glow emanated from the potion, and the three friends felt joy and fear in equal parts.

They approached the first statue, a young woman trapped in an eternal scream, and sprinkled the mixture over it. Immediately, the statue started to tremble and, before their eyes, the young stone woman came to life. Terrified, she turned away from them before disappearing into the night.

One by one, they repeated the process with every statue, releasing the trapped souls. However, as they went on, they began to hear malicious laughter all around them. The shadows in the garden seemed to move.

When they reached the last statue, a sinister-looking man caught in a pose of despair, Flavia hesitated. She recognised the figure, it was a man who tried to harm her long ago.

Suddenly they realised that the souls trapped in the statues were of evil people, who committed all sorts of heinous crimes, and were condemned to death. The three friends were surrounded by murderers that they freed themselves. They were not going to survive that night.

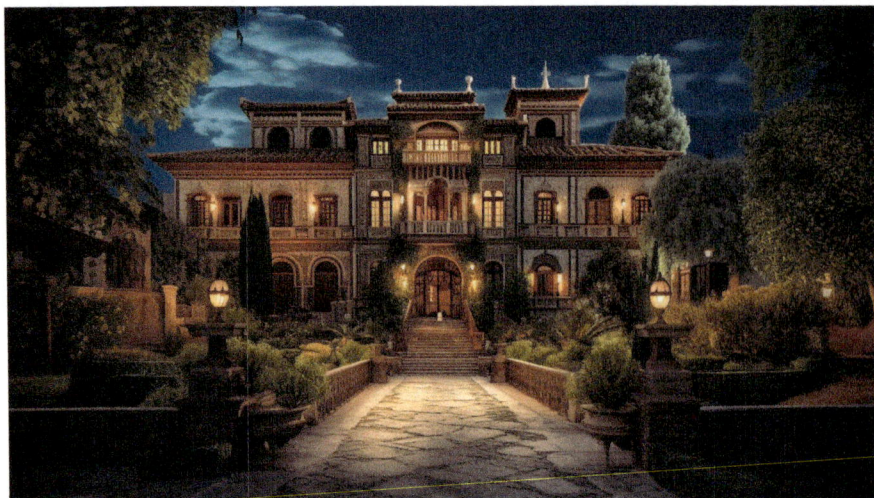

The mirror that devoured souls

The Mendoza mansion, located in the heart of Granada, was a refuge for Don Gaspar, a lover of the occult and the supernatural.

On one of his visits to the antiquarian, he found a finely carved gilt-framed mirror that caught his attention.

The old salesman warned him about the objects' dark history, but Don Gaspar, ignoring his warnings, decided to take it home.

Back at the mansion, Don Gaspar placed the mirror in his study, where he used to spend long hours researching and experimenting.

He soon realised that there was something special about the mirror: every time he looked at it, he felt a strange sense of unrest and unease, as if something dark and evil was hiding behind its surface.

Doña Maite, his wife, also started feeling uncomfortable in the house, without really knowing why. Nights became increasingly unbearable for her, as she swore hearing noises and moans coming from her husband's study.

Don Gaspar, convinced that the mirror was the key to her worries, began to investigate further into its origin and its supposed evil power.

Meanwhile, at the mansion, things were getting worse. Ricardo, the family servant, began to behave strangely, as if under the influence of some dark force. His gaze grew vacant and his attitude more distant.

Desperate, Doña Maite sought help from Father Francisco, the local priest, who, after hearing the story of the mirror, decided to visit the mansion to try and find out what evil had been unleashed in that home.

Father Francisco arrived at the Mendoza mansion with a resolute attitude and ready to face whatever evil dwelt in the place.

Doña Maite, relieved by the presence of the priest, took him to the study where the mirror was.

At the sight of it, Father Francisco felt the object reject him. The reflection turned strange, as if the study was an empty room. The priest knew at once that the mirror was wicked.

In the meantime, Don Gaspar, in his search for information, had found an ancient document that spoke of a cursed mirror, capable of devouring the souls of those who looked into it.

According to the document, the mirror had been created by a necromancer at the time of the Holy Inquisition, as a revenge against those who had condemned him for his dark arts. The mirror had been destroyed and its fragments scattered throughout Europe, but apparently someone rebuilt it.

Father Francisco, knowing that he had to act quickly, decided to bless the house in an attempt to free it from the evil influence of the mirror. However, during the ceremony, something went terribly wrong: the mirror seemed to be resisting the priest's blessing, and a dark shadow began to emerge from its surface, threatening to devour the soul of Father Francisco himself.

Right then Don Gaspar burst into the study. He dragged Doña Maite and Father Francisco out and told them what he discovered. The mirror must be destroyed and they had to find a way to do so before it could claim more souls.

Resolved to find a solution, they embarked on a desperate quest to discover how to destroy the mirror once and for all. At the mansion, Ricardo, the servant, was succumbing more and more to the dark influence of the cursed object.

Father Francisco took Don Gaspar and Doña Maite to the library of an old convent on the outskirts of the city. There, among dusty volumes and forgotten parchments, they hoped to find the key to free their lives from the terror that haunted them.

They spent whole days searching, increasingly desperate, while Ricardo fell into the clutches of the cursed mirror. The servant, once loyal and helpful, became gradually duller and erratic, disappearing for long hours for no apparent reason.

Finally, in the depths of the library, Don Gaspar found a manuscript that seemed to be the answer to their problems. The text, written in Latin and with Christian symbols in its margins, described a liturgy that, if performed correctly, would break the curse of the mirror and free the souls trapped inside. However, the liturgy required a sacred object that had been lost centuries ago: the Tear of Saint Ignatius, a crystal blessed by the saint on his deathbed.

With renewed hope and a new mission in mind, the trio left the convent library and embarked on a hunt for the sacred crystal. The search took them all over Spain, following clues and legends that led them to holy sites and places of pilgrimage. As they progressed, the time pressure became more stressful, knowing that till they found the Tear of Saint Ignatius, the mirror would continue to haunt and consume Ricardo and, eventually, all of them.

After months of tireless searching, they finally reached a small village in the mountains of northern Spain, where the Tear of Saint Ignatius was said to be last seen. There, in a dilapidated and almost forgotten church, they found the sacred crystal, hidden in a secret niche behind the high altar.

But Ricardo had already succumbed completely to the power of the cursed mirror. His soul had darkened and his face had become cadaverous. The servant, now a pawn of the mirror, started luring others into the mansion, where their souls were also devoured by the wicked object.

With the Tear of Saint Ignatius in their power, the trio returned to the mansion, where they were horrified to see the state of Ricardo and the other captives of the mirror, but they knew there was no time to lose.

Following the instructions of the ancient manuscript, they performed the liturgy. Doña Maite held the Tear of Saint Ignatius in front of the mirror, while Father Francisco recited the sacred words in Latin and Don Gaspar traced crosses on the floor with white chalk.

The mirror began shaking and emitting a deafening scream, as if all the souls trapped inside were crying out in unison. The Tear of Saint Ignatius shone brightly, and a blinding light filled the room.

The light intensified further and the piercing cry of the mirror became almost unbearable. Father Francisco continued to recite the sacred words, his voice strong and loud, while Doña Maite held the Tear of Saint Ignatius in steady hands. Don Gaspar, for his part, remained alert, protecting his companions.

Suddenly, the mirror exploded into a thousand pieces, releasing a whirlwind of trapped souls. The light of the Tear of Saint Ignatius seemed to guide them into the beyond, allowing them to find the peace that had been denied them. The servant and the other captives, released from the evil influence of the mirror, fell to the ground, dizzy but alive.

Ricardo lay pale and emaciated on the floor, Doña Maite ran to him, hugging him with tears in her eyes as the servant slowly regained consciousness. Father Francisco and Don Gaspar looked at each other, knowing they had achieved the impossible.

The mansion, once gloomy and sombre, was restored to its former splendour. The liberated souls took with them the blackness that had enveloped the house for so long. Don Gaspar continued his passion for the supernatural, but refrained from buying any more objects.

What became of the soul-devouring mirror was never known for certain, but its fragments had supposedly been scattered around the world, to ensure that it could never reassemble itself and unleash its horror. One of its fragments was left embedded that night in the wooden wall of Don Gaspar's study. It always went unnoticed.

Thirst for eternity

The carriage moved slowly along the winding road, surrounded by tall trees that seemed willing to embrace it. Jack Hartfield, a young London lawyer, watched the scenery with a mixture of anticipation and anxiety.

He had accepted a legal commission that took him to Romania, a land of ancient legends and mysteries, which aroused fascination and fear in equal measure.

The reason for his journey was a complicated legal matter involving the ownership of a castle in the Carpathian Mountains, whose past was shrouded in shadows and whose heirs were caught in a tangle of claims and disputes. His mind wandered with legal concerns as the carriage continued its slow progress.

At the end of the road, the figure of a woman emerged from the morning mist. Dressed in black, with dark hair that waved like the night, she looked like a vision. When the carriage stopped and Jack stepped out, the woman approached him, her beauty momentarily taking his breath away.

'Welcome to Romania, Mr. Hartfield!' she greeted in a soft, melodic voice that seemed to have a tinge of sadness in its tone. 'I am Mirela Dragulia, and I have come to greet you on behalf of the owner of the castle.'

Jack nodded and introduced himself cordially. As they gazed into each other's eyes, he felt an odd sensation that there was something more in Mirela's gaze, something inscrutable and mysterious. But before he could deepen that impression, a new carriage drawn by black horses appeared beside them.

'We must leave for the castle at once, Mr. Hartfield,' said Mirela, as the carriage waited before them. Night falls quickly in these lands, and it is not advisable to travel these roads after dark.

Jack nodded and climbed into the carriage with Mirela. As they drove through the dark Carpathian forest towards the castle, he couldn't help but feel that he was entering an unknown and mysterious world, where the shadows hid secrets waiting to be revealed.

Night was falling over Romania, and in the gloom, Mirela's figure seemed to fade like an ephemeral dream, while the castle, with its ominous gothic architecture, loomed in the distance, ready to reveal its own secrets.

The carriage stopped before the imposing iron gates of the castle. Jack felt small and insignificant in the sombre majesty of the structure that was raising before him. The Carpathian castle had an abject presence, as if steeped in a long and dark history.

Jack descended from the carriage and reached out to Mirela to help her down. Her touch was cold, almost icy, and Jack shivered, in a mixture of fear and seduction.

'Enter freely and of your own will, Mr. Hartfield,' said Mirela with a smile that seemed to fade into the shadows. 'The night is relentless here, and the castle offers shelter from its horrors.'

Jack followed Mirela through the heavy iron gates and they entered a gloomy foyer lit only by the dim light of torches. The walls were covered with antique tapestries and portraits of people with enigmatic looks. A resounding silence filled the air.

Soon, they were greeted by Lord Dimitri Dragulia, the owner of the castle. He was a middle-aged man with dark hair and piercing eyes. His countenance seemed marked by sadness, and his welcome to Jack was polite but distant.

'I thank you for coming, Mr. Hartfield,' said Dimitri as he shook Jack's hand. 'I hope our legal situation can be resolved promptly.'

Jack nodded and they began discussing the legal details in the castle study. In the meantime, he couldn't help but feel that something didn't quite fit. There was something unusual about the atmosphere of the place.

Later, after an austere dinner served by silent servants, Jack retired to his room. It was spacious and embellished with antique furniture. It struck him that there was no mirror.

As he prepared for bed, he heard murmurs and whispers that looked like coming from the castle walls themselves. Every time he tried to locate the source of the sounds, they stopped, as if shadows obscured their source.

Finally, Jack climbed into bed, but sleep did not come easily. The night was full of mysteries and secrets, and the thirst for eternity seemed to pulsate through the walls of the Carpathian castle.

The third night at the castle brought a full moon that illuminated the surrounding landscape. From his window, Jack could see the lush forests, stretching as far as the eye could see, and the mountains that appeared to touch the starry sky.

During the day, he continued his legal discussions with Dimitri, but the feeling of unease persisted. Mirela, the attractive young woman who brought him here, seemed to be everywhere, watching from the darkness with her piercing eyes.

That night, Jack decided to explore the castle for himself. He descended a stone staircase that appeared to lead him into the depths of the fortification. Torches along the corridor cast dancing shadows on the walls.

In a corner, Jack found a solid wooden door. He pushed it carefully and found himself in a room that looked like frozen in time.

It was filled with old portraits and strange objects. One of the portraits attracted his attention in particular: it showed a young woman who looked strikingly like Mirela. That made him think she might be an undead, he had heard legends about Nosferatu, *das vampire*... Could they be true?

As Jack scanned the room, a soft voice startled him.

'What are you doing here, Mr. Hartfield?' It was Mirela, appearing out of nowhere like a spectre. Her eyes glowed in the gloom.

'I was exploring,' Jack stammered nervously. 'This castle is so intriguing, full of history.'

Mirela approached him with unearthly grace.

'The history of this castle is older than you can imagine, Mr. Hartfield. And it is full of secrets that some would wish to forget.'

Jack looked at her with a mixture of dread and desire.

'What secrets are these?'

Mirela smiled, but her smile seemed devoid of warmth.

'Blood secrets, Mr. Hartfield. Secrets that have been guarded for centuries and that only a few can comprehend.'

Before Jack could ask any more questions, Mirela vanished into the shadows, leaving him alone in the mystery-filled room.

Fear took hold of him as he began to understand that he had fallen into an enigma far more sinister than he could ever imagine.

The days at the castle passed slowly, as Jack continued his interactions with Dimitri Dragulia and the enigmatic Mirela.

Each night, Mirela visited him in his dreams, whispering promises of eternity and power. Despite his initial fear, Jack found himself increasingly drawn to her - she was, after all, a gorgeous young woman.

On a cloudy afternoon, Dimitri took him to a secret room in one of the castle's towers. The room was filled with ancient tomes and dusty scrolls.

Dimitri explained that they contained the ancestral knowledge of his lineage, including processes they could undertake to obtain immortality.

Jack was hesitant, but his obsession with immortality drove him on.

Dimitri offered him a sinister pact: he would have to surrender his soul to darkness in exchange for eternal life. All it required was a little of his blood. Jack's heart pounded as he held the quill and parchment. Mirela stood in the corner of the room, watching silently. Her eyes glowed with inhuman lust.

Jack decided not to continue the conversation and retired to his room. Mirela, the seductive vampire, continued to visit him frequently in his dreams. Their nocturnal encounters were a dangerous dance between desire and terror. Jack could not resist her attraction, but at the same time, he knew that she would be the cause of his perdition.

One night, while he wandered through the dark corridors of the castle, he heard a distant wail that drew him to an ancient crypt.

When he entered, he found a grisly scene: several bloodless bodies lay on the floor, their eyes wide open in eternal terror.

Mirela stood in the centre of the crypt, a satisfied expression on her face. Her arms and white dress were stained with blood.

'Jack, darling, you're just in time,' she whispered.

The sight of the massacre filled him with horror, but something within him was drawn to the grotesque scene.

'Join us,' Mirela urged him, extending a pale, bloodied hand towards him. 'Only then can you reach true eternity.'

The choice hung over Jack like the sword of Damocles. The crypt, soaked with the blood of the victims, exuded a mixture of temptation and horror that paralysed him. Mirela's eyes stared at him with hypnotic intensity, as if she could read his deepest thoughts.

'Eternity awaits, Jack,' Mirela whispered with an enigmatic smile. 'Together we can conquer the world of the shadows. No more human fears nor weaknesses.'

Jack, seduced by Mirela's beauty, allows himself to be guided to a coffin in the room. The vampire pushes Jack into the coffin and stands over him. She kisses him passionately and then quickly throws herself on his neck. As Mirela draws his blood, Jack feels a mixture of pain and pleasure. Slowly, the poison takes hold of him. Once Mirela is sated, she gets up and withdraws from the crypt, leaving Jack motionless in the coffin.

After a few hours, Jack wakes up. He is no longer the same. He knows he has become one of them. Fear seizes him, but the idea of living forever pleases him.

At that moment, he remembers his family, his wife and children who were left behind in the world of the living. The image of his youngest son, with his eyes full of innocence, becomes unbearable.

He decides to go back to his life and hide the fact that he is a vampire. He gathers his things and sets out to return to his home. The heavy door closes behind him, and the gloomy castle is left behind.

After days of travelling, Jack arrives home in London, where his wife greets him warmly. She doesn't seem to notice anything. The children don't notice anything either. Maybe everything is fine. Maybe Jack can lead a normal life.

When night falls, they go to bed. The woman begins to touch Jack affectionately, but he no longer sees her as he used to, he wants something different from her: her blood.

If you liked the book, don't forget to:

🎃 Leave a good review on Amazon.

🎃 Follow the author's news at afsoria.com

Printed in Dunstable, United Kingdom